"I'll stay the night," he said in a gruff voice.

Sarah's lips parted to mouth the word "What?"

"I said I'll stay the night."

She shook her head, her mind racing. She grabbed her Palm Pilot and wrote, "No."

"Look, Sarah, you may think this was a random burglar, but I don't. Think about it. That story came out about you overhearing a kidnapping, and someone breaks in to your apartment and attacks you all in the same day. Too coincidental for me."

Fear seeped back inside her, chilling her to the bone. "But you don't need to stay—"

"You don't have to be afraid of me, Sarah." He cleared his throat. "I know I was out of line earlier, and I told you it won't happen again. But I will keep you safe."

Sarah's heart fluttered. He'd keep her safe from danger, but who would protect her from him?

Dear Harlequin Intrigue Reader,

We've got another explosive lineup of four thrilling titles for you this month. Like you'd expect anything less of Harlequin Intrigue—*the* line for breathtaking romantic suspense.

Sylvie Kurtz returns to east Texas in *Red Thunder Reckoning* to conclude her emotional story of the Makepeace brothers in her two-book FLESH AND BLOOD series. Dani Sinclair takes *Scarlet Vows* in the third title of our modern Gothic continuity, MORIAH'S LANDING. Next month you can catch Joanna Wayne's exciting series resolution in *Behind the Veil*.

The agents at Debra Webb's COLBY AGENCY are taking appointments this month—fortunately for one woman who's in serious jeopardy. But with a heartthrob Latino bodyguard for protection, it's uncertain who poses the most danger—the killer *or* her *Personal Protector*.

Finally, in a truly innovative story, Rita Herron brings us to NIGHTHAWK ISLAND. When one woman's hearing is restored by an experimental surgery, she's awakened to the sound of murder in *Silent Surrender*. But only one hardened detective believes her. And only he can guard her from certain death.

So don't forget to pick up all four for a complete reading experience. Enjoy!

Sincerely,

Denise O'Sullivan
Associate Senior Editor
Harlequin Intrigue

SILENT SURRENDER

RITA HERRON

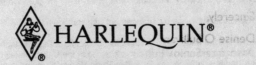

HARLEQUIN®

TORONTO • NEW YORK • LONDON
AMSTERDAM • PARIS • SYDNEY • HAMBURG
STOCKHOLM • ATHENS • TOKYO • MILAN • MADRID
PRAGUE • WARSAW • BUDAPEST • AUCKLAND

ISBN 0-373-22660-8

SILENT SURRENDER

Visit us at www.eHarlequin.com

Printed in U.S.A.

ABOUT THE AUTHOR

Rita Herron is a teacher, workshop leader and storyteller who loves reading, writing and sharing stories with people of all ages. She has published two nonfiction books for adults on working and playing with children, and has won the Golden Heart award for a young adult story. Rita believes that books taught her to dream, and she loves nothing better than sharing that magic with others. She lives with her dream husband and three children, two cats and a dog in Norcross, Georgia. Rita loves to hear from readers. You can contact her at www.ritaherron.com or P.O. Box 921225, Norcross, GA 30092.

Books by Rita Herron

HARLEQUIN INTRIGUE
486—SEND ME A HERO
523—HER EYEWITNESS
556—FORGOTTEN LULLABY
601—SAVING HIS SON
660—SILENT SURRENDER†

HARLEQUIN AMERICAN ROMANCE
820—HIS-AND-HERS TWINS
859—HAVE GOWN, NEED GROOM*
872—HAVE BABY, NEED BEAU*
883—HAVE HUSBAND, NEED HONEYMOON*

*The Hartwell Hope Chests
†Nighthawk Island

Don't miss any of our special offers. Write to us at the following address for information on our newest releases.

Harlequin Reader Service
U.S.: 3010 Walden Ave., P.O. Box 1325, Buffalo, NY 14269
Canadian: P.O. Box 609, Fort Erie, Ont. L2A 5X3

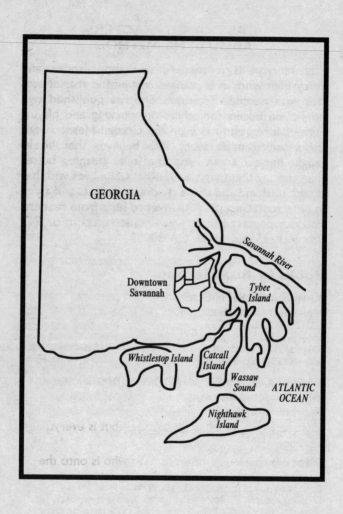

GEORGIA

Savannah River

Downtown
Savannah

Tybee
Island

Whistlestop Island

Catcall
Island

Wassaw
Sound

ATLANTIC
OCEAN

Nighthawk
Island

CAST OF CHARACTERS

Sarah Cutter—A deaf woman who has lived in silence for twenty years regains her hearing only to hear the terrifying sounds of a woman's desperate cry as she is being kidnapped. When she tells the police her bizarre story, she suddenly finds herself running for her life and facing the biggest fear of all—losing her heart to her protector, Adam Black.

Adam Black—A jaded cop who must accept Sarah Cutter's bizarre story and protect her life in order to find his missing sister, but can he protect himself from falling in love with the tempting but vulnerable woman?

Denise Black Harley—Adam's missing sister is a doctor on the verge of a brilliant discovery that could help mankind—or get her killed.

Russell Harley—Denise's estranged husband has hard feelings about the separation, but is he bitter enough to seek revenge?

Sol Santenelli—Sarah's godfather—he saved her life once and loves her more than anything—or does he?

Charles Cutter—Sarah's father—a research scientist who murdered his own wife and almost killed his daughter twenty years ago so he could sell his secret discovery to a foreign government—but is everything as it seems?

Robey Burgess—A nosy reporter who is onto the story of a lifetime—will he break the story in time to earn his fame or die trying?

Arnold Hughes—This former military man and the CEO and cofounder of the research park was a close friend of Sarah's father—or was he?

To Denise O'Sullivan,
for asking for something different…hope you enjoy.

Prologue

A loud explosion rumbled through the house. Five-year-old Sarah Cutter clutched her tattered blanket to her chest and tried not to cry. She *hated* thunderstorms. Especially lightning.

Suddenly the walls erupted into flames and she screamed.

"There's a bomb!" her mother yelled. "Run, Sarah, get out!"

Sarah bolted off the sofa, dashing toward the kitchen and her mother, but another loud explosion rocked the floor beneath her, and she stumbled and fell. Glass and wood shattered around her. Jagged shards stabbed her face and arms, and flames shot into the doorway in front of her.

"Mommy, help!"

Smoke stung her eyes, so thick it billowed around her, clogging her vision. Then her mother's blurred figure staggered into the doorway, flames eating at her clothes. Sarah stretched out her arms. But instead of grabbing her, her mother shoved her backward. "Run, honey, get out! Now!"

Another boom tore through the house, and the roof collapsed on top of her mother, sending blood trailing down her forehead. Tears streamed down Sarah's cheeks. She had to save her mother. She crawled forward, but heat scalded her knees, and glass slivers jabbed her palms. The fire was gobbling the wood floor, hissing like a monster!

More wood splintered and rained down, pelting Sarah's body. She covered her head with her hands and searched for her father. She saw him through the window. He was outside. He would save them!

But another board smacked her temple and pain exploded in her head. Then silence came, as swift and jarring as the darkness that sucked her into its big dark hole.

A sudden deafening silence.

Chapter One

Twenty years later

Today Sarah's sentence of silence would finally end.

She struggled to pull herself from the deep sleep of the anesthesia. If she could open her eyes and focus, she would be able to hear again. Hear the beautiful sounds of music. Voices. Laughter.

Her fingers and toes tingled and her arms felt heavy, but slowly she moved one hand. In even slower degrees, she opened her heavy eyelids and finally brought her surroundings into focus. The doctor's warnings rose in her mind: *Don't expect miracles. You had a lot of scar tissue to remove, and will have some swelling that will take time to go down. You may experience some pain and discomfort, some warbled sounds. And it'll take time for your brain to retrain itself to interpret sounds. Be patient.*

She'd been patient for twenty years, waiting on the right doctor, on advances in technology to produce a sophisticated hearing implant that could restore her hearing. Finally good news had come.

Her godfather, Sol Santenelli sat hunched over,

asleep in the chair in the corner, his scruffy gray beard and hair sticking out as if he'd run his hands through it a thousand times. Dear sweet Sol. What would she have done without him?

He'd taken care of her after her parents had died in the explosion, and then when she'd struggled with her deafness. And when she'd been unable to speak after the fire, he'd called in a specialist. Once her vocal cords had healed from the smoke damage, the doctors hadn't found any physical reason for her lack of speech; they'd blamed it on trauma. And when she was old enough to understand, that her father had actually set off the explosion and killed her mother, Sol had held her while she'd cried.

She wanted him to wake and talk to her, wanted to hear his voice again.

A sound suddenly burst through her consciousness, and Sarah's fingers tightened around the hospital bed. The special hearing implant was actually working—she would hear again.

She strained for another sound. A voice maybe. Someone walking? A door closing?

But suddenly a piercing pain shot through her temple. She pressed her hand over her ears, tears filling her eyes. The pain was excruciating, triggering nausea in her stomach. Seconds later, a muffled cry broke through the pain—the sound of another scream. Just like the sound her mother had made before she died.

Her heart squeezing, Sarah searched the room for the woman, but it was empty, except for Sol. Where had the scream come from? The hallway maybe? Another room? Dr. Tucker had suggested her hearing might be more acute than a normal person's because of the high-tech implant, but she hadn't believed him, hadn't been able to imagine hearing sounds—

The voice broke through again, "Where are you taking me?"

"Just shut up, Dr. H—" Static cut in, making the words garbled, "—ardy a…nd do as w…e say."

"No!" The woman cried out again as if she were struggling to escape.

"I said sh…ut up or y…ou die." A harsh smacking sound, then a dull thud followed.

The man had hit the woman, Sarah realized, a chill rippling up her spine. She must have fallen to the floor. Was the woman dead? Being kidnapped?

Confusion clouded Sarah's brain. She was in the hospital, so where was the woman? In the hall? The room next door? Was she a nurse? A patient? Another doctor?

She gripped the bed rail again and struggled to get up. She had to get help. Had to tell someone. But her limbs were too heavy to lift. She tried to speak, but her voice squeaked, so she pounded on the bed rail, shaking it to wake her godfather.

Seconds later, he stood by her side, smiling, tucking her hair behind her ears with his bony fingers, his gray eyes full of concern and love. She raised her hand enough to sign, describing the incident.

"Honey, you had to be dreaming. You've been under anesthesia. The drugs can do funny things to your mind."

His voice sounded like heaven, thick and deep and slightly hoarse with emotions just as she'd imagined. He squeezed her hand, and she smiled at the unfamiliar stubble on his jaw, wishing she could verbalize how much the sound of his voice meant.

"You can hear me, can't you love?"

Sarah nodded, her throat clogging at the moisture she saw glistening in his eyes. Maybe he was right. Maybe she'd imagined the woman's scream. She'd probably been dreaming about the explosion that had killed her parents and had heard the haunting memory of her mother's cry.

But the sound of the woman's scream echoed in her mind as she drifted back to sleep. And she couldn't help but wonder if there really had been a woman in danger somewhere in the building. If so, who was she and what had happened to her?

Three days later

"I THINK MY sister is missing." Detective Adam Black, Savannah Police Department, paced a wide circle around his desk, glaring at the mounds of paperwork he had yet to do. But he couldn't think about mundane tasks right now. He had to find Denise.

His partner, Clayton Fox, stared up at him with a frown. "Look, Black, don't go jumping to conclusions."

Shoving aside a half-empty cup of coffee, Adam grabbed the phone and punched in her number. He let the phone ring a dozen times, then slammed it down in frustration. "Where the hell is she? I've been calling her for three days and she hasn't answered or returned my calls."

"Did you try to reach her at work?"

"Of course. The secretary at the research center said she went on vacation, but Denise never goes anywhere without telling me. Something's wrong." He gripped the desk edge with white-knuckled fists. "She's in trouble somewhere, Clay, I can feel it."

Clayton's black eyebrows rose. "Have you checked with her friends? Her husband?"

Adam nodded. "Denise and Russell are separated. He claims he hasn't talked to her in weeks. And she's not close with anybody else that I know of. Since the separation she's been spending all her time at the research center."

"Do you know what she's working on?"

"No. Most of those damn projects are so top secret I wonder if the scientists even know what they're involved in."

"Maybe she's absorbed in her research, staying late—"

"Sleeping at the office?"

Clayton shrugged but Adam shook his head. "She'd still check in."

A moment of real concern darkened his partner's eyes. "Have you checked the hospitals then…"

He let the sentence trail off and Adam understood the implication. The hospitals, the morgue… "Yeah. But I'm checking again."

"I'll get busy with that paperwork for the captain."

Adam nodded his thanks, his chest tightening as he scanned the police reports for victims, deaths or hospital injuries that might point to her whereabouts. He breathed a sigh of relief when he hung up from the morgue. Thank God, he hadn't found her name or anyone fitting her description.

Phones pealed around him, computers hummed away and loud voices sounded from the captain's office. He'd drive over to Denise's and see if she was home. Maybe she had the flu and wasn't answering her phone.

But the door swung open and in walked a frail-looking woman, triggering a hum of silence across the room. All the male cops immediately sized her up, Adam included. She was a hell of a looker, about five-four, slender frame but generous chested, delicate heart-shaped face with pale porcelain skin that looked like it belonged on a doll and hair so black it resembled charcoal. Her eyes were almond shaped, the color a vivid, startling blue that reminded him of the sky after a heavy thunderstorm. And her lips were full and pink like ripe raspberries.

He fisted his hands by his side, shaken at his response.

She scanned the room, her gaze meeting his, and heat curled low in his belly. The pull was there, hot and sudden, a feeling that hadn't happened to him in a long time. As if she felt the charge between them and was afraid of it, she jerked her gaze away, and headed toward one of the female officers. Probably thought Bernstein less intimidating because she was a woman. But she was wrong. Bernstein had a soft spot for no one.

Clayton loped toward the woman. Adam dug in his pocket for his keys, then mumbled a curse when Clayton motioned for him to join them in one of the interrogation rooms.

Several minutes later, after Clay had introduced the two of them, Adam stared in surprise as the woman scribbled a message on a Palm Pilot. Her name was Sarah, soft and sexy just like her. But her last name was Cutter, a bit sharp, although it mirrored the wariness in her eyes.

She claimed she'd been in the hospital three days before and had overheard a woman scream for help.

"What woman?" Clayton asked.

"And why the Palm Pilot?" Adam indicated the small computer.

She bit down on her lip, drawing his attention to the delicate curve of her chin and the vulnerable shadows that haunted her face. He didn't want to feel sorry for her, but judging from the dark smudges beneath her eyes, she'd been through hell and back. He wondered if she was sick, then wanted to kick himself for being concerned. He knew better than to get involved.

He had his own damn problems.

"I don't speak well," she wrote. "I lost my hearing when I was five."

"But you can hear now?" he asked. She'd frowned when he'd spoken, her eyes creasing together as if she'd had to concentrate to understand him. And she kept staring at his mouth while he talked as if she might be reading his lips. Or maybe she was just too afraid to look into his eyes again.

In any case, he found himself fixated on *her* mouth, on those kissable lips, and he didn't like it.

"Yes, I recently had surgery and received hearing implants."

Ahh. He arched a brow and waited for her to continue. When she didn't, Clayton spoke up, "Okay, tell us exactly what you heard."

She scribbled, "I don't know who the woman was. I heard her cry out, then decided I must have imagined it. But I've heard her voice again, twice this week."

"Did you tell someone in the hospital about the woman?" Clayton asked.

"Yes." Her mouth formed the word silently. "My godfather. He suggested I'd been dreaming because of the medication. But the more I think about it, the more I know I was awake. The people must have been down the hall or in the next room or outside the window."

Clayton rocked the wooden chair back on two legs. "You're saying you heard a woman being kidnapped but nobody else in the building heard it except you? What are you, a psychic or something?"

Adam bit back a chuckle at the disbelief in his partner's voice.

She shook her head, a spark of anger lighting her eyes while she fidgeted with a silver locket around her neck. Finally she turned to Adam and met his gaze again, as if she wanted to see if the connection was still there, if *he'd* believe her. It was, the sliver of awareness tingling along his nerve endings, but he steeled himself against any emotion.

She finally tore her gaze from his and wrote, "Yes, but my godfather Sol convinced me the anesthesia had affected me. After I went home, though, I heard the voices again. One night, it was late, the man and woman were arguing...." She shuddered as if the memories were too painful to revisit. Adam had the insane urge to fold her in his arms and comfort her like he used to do his sister when she was little and woke from a nightmare.

"Wait a minute." Clayton held up a hand to stop her. "First you heard the voices at the hospital, then at home? How close do you live to the hospital?"

A shadow passed over her eyes. "About ten miles."

Adam thumbed his hair from his face, impatience

flaring at himself for being attracted to her. This woman was some kind of psycho, wasting their time. Clayton shot him a sideways grin as if he had read his mind and agreed.

"Were you sleeping when you heard them?" Clayton asked in a soft tone.

"Yes, but I woke up with this strange piercing sound in my ear. Then I heard the man and woman arguing. The man was forcing her to go somewhere with him."

"And these were the same people you heard at the hospital?" Clayton asked.

She nodded.

"Did you recognize the voices?"

She glared at Clayton. "I told you I just got my hearing back, so, no, I hadn't heard the voices before."

Adam almost smiled at her small show of spunk. "Listen, ma'am, it's a stretch to think you heard something strange go down at the hospital," Clayton said, "but to hear those same voices again miles away from the hospital at your house, that's impossible. Have you ever heard voices in your head before?"

The woman sounded schizophrenic, Adam decided.

She shook her head no again, and those vibrant blue eyes swung Adam's way to see his reaction. Bizarre as it sounded, he found himself trying to make some sense of her story. Could her hearing implant somehow work like a radio transmitter?

She hesitated as if she had a moment of sanity and realized how crazy she sounded, then gave him a pleading look. "I received an experimental type of hearing implant at the research center. The doctor said my hearing might be warbled at times, more acute at others, and in the beginning it might sometimes be delayed.''

"Delayed hearing? A special hearing implant that allows you to hear through walls?'' *She was a candidate for the nuthouse.* Adam pointed to himself, then Clayton. "Could you hear everyone else on the street talking? How about us—did you hear us talking from your house, too? Is that why you came here?'' He stood, annoyed at himself for being suckered in and wanting to believe her when he should be looking for Denise.

"Are you saying you have some kind of bionic ear?'' Clayton asked.

She stood this time and closed her eyes briefly as if to regain control. When she opened her eyes, her expression bordered on panic. She knew her story sounded crazy yet she'd come anyway. Why?

And she was looking at Adam, all sad-eyed and sincere and fiercely determined to make him believe her. She had so much depth there—it was almost as if she could see inside him, smell the cold distance he put between himself and everyone else in the world. The distance he had to keep in order to survive.

Shaken, he looked away and stared at the window, purposely raised his chin so he wouldn't have to look into those soulful eyes. So he wouldn't have to see the slight tremble in her hands, the quiver of that bottom lip. So his body wouldn't stir at the soft vulnerability in her feminine form.

So he wouldn't reach out and touch her.

This was the wrong damn woman to even think about jumping in bed with. She needed psychotherapy instead of a detective. He turned and opened his mouth to tell her that but his partner cut him off.

"How did you lose your hearing, Ms. Cutter?" Clayton propped one leg on the battered table between them and leaned forward, his tone sympathetic.

A moment of anguish glittered in her eyes. Adam watched her fold her delicate hands, noticed the way she'd chewed her nails down to stubs, saw the faint scars along her palms and saw another one at the edge of her hairline, and all his protective instincts kicked in. What exactly had happened to her? Had she been in an accident? The scars looked faded and old, but she immediately dragged a strand of that ebony hair over the spot as if to hide it. Had she been victimized recently or early in her life?

"That isn't important," she replied. "What's important is that I heard a woman in trouble and you need to find her."

Clayton lowered his voice to a placating tone, "Look, I can understand your concern, but you have to give us more to go on than this. If a woman was in danger at the hospital, don't you think someone on staff would have heard, too?"

She shrugged as if she had no answers, only questions.

Stupid questions and a crazy story that no one would believe.

Denise's face flashed through Adam's mind, and he glanced at the clock, worry knotting his stomach. He had time for no one but Denise and his job. "Why don't you wait outside and we'll discuss this?"

She snatched her Palm Pilot and stalked from the office, her head held high.

Adam shook his head in pity as he watched her go,

dismissing the sexual draw that made him itch to go after her.

Still, he couldn't help himself—when she closed the door, he found himself wondering what her voice would sound like.

SARAH FOUGHT for a steadying breath as she leaned against the closed door. Several police officers and one seedy prisoner in a vulgar T-shirt handcuffed to a chair stared at her.

The detectives obviously hadn't believed her.

In fact, she could hear them laughing through the door.

She supposed she couldn't blame them—her story did sound bizarre. But it had happened. And those men, even her godfather, couldn't convince her otherwise. Sol. She'd thought he of all people would have supported her. But he'd reiterated the doctor's warnings about her brain having trouble interpreting sounds at first, the delayed translation between the sound and her interpretation, then his theory about the effects of anesthesia. He'd even suggested the surgery had resurrected repressed memories of the explosion that had caused her hearing loss and suggested she talk to a psychiatrist.

Another shudder passed through her as she heard Detective Black's gruff voice. She'd never met a more masculine man, one who radiated such stark power. He'd watched her with an intensity that had burned straight to her core.

She'd never felt that kind of heat from a man before.

It was the very reason his laughter had hurt so much. She'd been ridiculed as a child. Without her hearing, she'd learned to read nonverbal facial and body gestures, little nuances that others never even noticed. The very reason she'd felt such a strong attraction toward him. The reason she'd avoided his gaze. The sultry heat charging the air between them had been too electric.

Why had he been irritated at her, though? Because he saw her as weak? Didn't he realize she was trying to help save this poor woman?

"That broad must have come from the psych ward," she heard the detective named Fox say through the door. "She was beautiful, but crazy."

A curse word erupted from Detective Black's mouth, burning her ears through the walls. She could almost see those wide cheekbones tighten, his naturally dark skin glisten with sweat as his anger mounted. "A sexy one, but you're right, she needs medication. And what about that closed mouth? If she'd been able to hear until she was five, surely she had developed some speech."

"Yeah, more than a little weird."

She fought not to let the humiliation overwhelm her, but childhood memories of being taunted surfaced, clawing at her self-control again. Sol had been disappointed she hadn't instantly regained her speech when her hearing returned. Another reason he wanted her in therapy.

She moved toward the front of the station house, ignoring the curious looks. A tall, lanky man wearing khakis and wire-rimmed glasses bent to drink from the water fountain. He looked faintly familiar, as if she'd seen him when she was in the hospital. No, it couldn't have been. Yet, he watched her as she crossed the room and she did remember him. He was the reporter who'd confronted her outside the hospital wanting an interview about her hearing implant. He'd known about the explosion that had caused her hearing loss, and all about her father. So many ghosts to deal with...

Had he followed her here?

She squared her shoulders and ignored him, then strode toward the female officer's desk. Sarah swallowed, angling herself so the reporter couldn't see her.

"Can I help you?" the woman asked.

Sarah nodded, took a pen and paper from the officer's desk, then scribbled a few lines. She hesitated, continued writing, then handed the note to the other woman.

The officer frowned at her message just as the two detectives emerged from the back. Sarah walked out the door, struggling not to reveal her emotions as their laughter boomed behind her down the hall.

Seconds later, she entered the darkened parking deck, shivering at the early-afternoon shadows hovering around the concrete structure. As usual, she hesitated, gave her eyes a moment to adjust to the dimness and scanned the interior for strangers, wielding her keys between her fingers in case someone tried to grab her. She wasn't paranoid, but any female alone in the city had to play it safe, especially a deaf one. Her other senses had to make up for her lack of being able to hear someone approach.

The acrid smell of garbage seeped into her nostrils and the clattering of something—an aluminum can maybe—sent goose bumps up her arms. Another rattling sound broke the strained silence. Keys? Footsteps? Traffic noises, a hushed voice, a scrape. The different sounds bombarded her, disorienting her as to their proximity. She searched the darkness, found her car and headed straight toward it, almost running. Down two aisles, over beside the far wall. Only two more rows to go.

Her breath caught in her throat when she spotted a dark van parked beside her Jetta. She'd heard a news report say vans were the primary vehicle used for abductions.

She heard a clickety-clack sound and froze, then resumed walking and realized the sound had come from her own heels. Deciding she'd let the past few days rattle her, she slowed her steps. But a shadow caught her eye. Something had moved. A cat maybe? Somebody lurking behind one of the boulders?

She glanced to her left, quickly cutting a path around the van, her gaze scanning the area around it in case someone was hiding there. Laughter echoed off the concrete walls behind her and she tensed. The sound reminded her of the detective's harsh laughter. His mocking words ran through her mind, distracting her momentarily, and she stumbled over the drain and dropped her keys. Cursing, she knelt to grab them when a shuffling noise reverberated behind her. Then a pair of black shoes suddenly appeared, and a man's hand reached out for her.

Chapter Two

A tall lanky man rushed out the door behind Sarah Cutter. The skinny guy had been eyeballing her from the corner, but Adam hadn't thought much of it at the time. After all, oddballs drifted in and out of the precinct at all hours, reporting crimes, claiming to be victims, sometimes admitting to crimes they hadn't committed just to get attention. Was the man following Sarah Cutter?

Bernstein handed Clay a note. Clay studied it while Adam retrieved his gun to go to Denise's. Just as he made it to the door, his partner caught him.

"Hey, Black, what's your sister's married name?"

"Harley, why?"

Clayton held out his hand, a note tucked between his fingers. "Maybe you'd better take a look at this."

Adam glanced at the hastily scribbled message: "Check to see if a doctor named Hardy or Harper, something like that, works at the Coastal Island Research Park on Catcall Island. Make sure she's okay. Tell the other detectives the weird broad from the psych ward doesn't need medication. She's trying to save a woman's life."

Adam's breath caught in his lungs. How had the

woman heard their conversation through the closed door? He reread the note. Hardy, Harper—Harley? Was it possible? Could Sarah Cutter have been talking about his sister?

Sarah opened her mouth to scream but the only sound that emerged was a low gurgle. Her heart pounding, she twirled around and pushed at the man's hand, ready to raise a knee to his groin.

The scrawny reporter stood in the shadows, surveying her with his beady eyes as if she were his prey. He swiped her keys from the ground and held them by his side. "Wait, Ms. Cutter, I'm Robey Burgess from the *Savannah Times*."

She pursed her lips, fury welling inside. How dare he scare her like that? For once in her life, she wished she could make her voice work just so she could give him a piece of her mind. She opened her mouth again to do that when she heard her own thick, almost childlike squeak.

"I—I just want an interview," he stammered. "I've been trying to reach you for days. Why don't we go someplace and talk?"

His nasally voice sounded unpleasant, and the look of avid curiosity in his eyes reminded her of all the taunting she'd received as a child. This man knew about her past, about her father. He wanted to write about her in the paper as if she were some sideshow freak in a circus.

She shook her head and mouthed "Go Away," yanked the keys from his hand, then spun around and crossed the distance to her car. She was sliding inside when he caught her, wedged a hand in between her and the door, and stopped her from shutting it.

"I'm going to find out everything I can about you and what's going on at that research center," he said, "so you might as well talk to me."

She glared at him, her chest constricting. What did he mean? What was going on at the research center?

She held up a hand as if to ask him to wait a second, grabbed her Palm Pilot and wrote, "If you want to talk about the Coastal Island Research Park, talk to my godfather, Sol Santenelli. He's the director. Leave me alone."

"No. You know something's going on. That's the reason you went to the police." A nasty sneer covered his face. "Since *they* didn't believe you, maybe you should try me. I might take your story more seriously than the cops did. And I know all about Cutter's Crossing."

Sarah flinched. The term had been coined by the local scientific community after her father to symbolize the point where a doctor or scientist crossed the line between noble, ethical practices and unethical ones.

She didn't like this man, didn't trust him, and refused to have herself and Sol, the only family she had left, dragged through the papers. "I asked you to leave me alone," she wrote. "If you don't let go of that door right now, I'll hit my panic alarm."

His irritated gaze flickered over her, sending an uneasy feeling up her spine, but he released the door. "This isn't over, Ms. Cutter," he said in a low growl.

She slammed the door, tore out of the parking spot and wound through the parking deck on screeching tires, checking over her shoulder to see if he followed her.

ADAM RACED OUTSIDE to the parking lot. He had to talk to that Cutter woman again. But just as he reached the first row of cars, a red Jetta flew round the corner on two wheels. A swirl of black hair flashed in his eyes and he realized the driver was Sarah Cutter. She was tearing from the lot as if death rode on her heels.

Knowing he couldn't catch her, he memorized her license plate, then headed to his car and radioed back inside to find out where she lived. While he waited for her address, he'd swing by the research center.

Although it was past five, his sister never adhered to a nine-to-five schedule. Maybe he'd find Denise there now, totally immersed in test tubes and cultures, obsessed with a new discovery or near breakthrough. Then he could breathe easily again. And forget about Sarah Cutter's bizarre story. And those bewitching eyes…

He crossed the bridge to Catcall Island, inhaling the salty air and pungent odor of the marshland. Catcall Island was the main hub of CIRP, the Coastal Island Research Park. The island had been given its name because locals claimed the sea oats were so thick in the marsh that when a wind came through, it sounded like a cat's low cry. On the map, Catcall resembled the shape of an old woman's shoe. The Institute of Oceanography and main campus were located near the tip of the island with some mountainous parts farther north, the toe of the shoe, with residential areas in the middle, and the marshland at the base. A smaller group of facilities had been housed on the neighboring Whistlestop Island, with future development planned there.

He frowned at the name—Whistlestop had garnered its name from an old ghost tale about a sea captain who lost his bride to a pirate during the turn of the century. Legend claimed the sea captain rode the coastal waters for years, grieving for her, whistling her favorite love ballad as he searched. Locals said she was his one true love, that he vowed not to stop whistling until he found her. Some still insist that they'd heard him whistling late at night when they'd been on the water.

A bunch of romantic gibberish.

A few miles to the south of Whistlestop lay the third island, Nighthawk Island, a smaller piece of land shrouded with such thick mist and fog that it appeared dark and eerie, almost twilight twenty-four hours a day. An ancient legend told about an unusual breed of dark-red legged hawks that inhabited the island; the nighthawks preyed on weaker animals, and had also been known to attack people. Supposedly, secret government-funded projects were conducted there. The island was guarded by a strict private agency called Seaside Securities—an innocuous name that seemed deceptive in view of the classified research projects conducted under its realm.

Three years ago the Savannah Economic Development Group had joined forces with several environmental agencies, universities and the governor, and pushed to grow the economy by plotting a research park similar to the Research Triangle Park in the Raleigh-Durham area in North Carolina. Since then, several pharmaceutical and medical research companies as well as microbiologists and marine biologists had relocated on Catcall, along with some government and university funded research projects. Some were affiliated with university projects and Savannah Hospital. Adam didn't know what type of research his sister was working on at the moment, but it had something to do with neurology.

Rain drizzled from the sky as he parked in front of Denise's building and hurried inside. A thin young brunette with a severe eyebrow line and a brown knot of hair on top of her head turned from her computer. "May I help you?"

"I'm here to see Dr. Harley."

A moment of apprehension flashed in her eyes. "She's not here."

"Look, Miss—" he paused and read her nameplate "—Johnson, Dr. Harley is my sister. I've been trying to reach her for days and she hasn't returned my calls. It's important I talk to her."

"I believe she went on vacation." She checked the calendar on her desk. "Yes, she's been penciled out for two weeks."

"That's impossible," Adam said. "She wouldn't have left town without telling me."

She tugged the beads around her neck. "I'm sorry, sir, but Dr. Bradford said she phoned to say she was going away for a few days."

Adam's hand tightened around the woman's polished desk. "Then she must have left a number where she can be reached."

She shuffled the files on her desk. "No, I don't believe so."

"Not even with Bradford?"

"Not that I know of."

"Let me see him."

"He's not here, either."

Adam gritted his teeth. "Where can I reach him?"

She glanced at her calendar again, looking impatient. "He's also out for a couple of days. I'll tell him to phone you if he calls in."

Adam handed her a business card and watched her eyes widen with alarm at his identity. "That's Detective Black," he said in a hard voice. "Is there anyone else from her department I can talk to?"

She glanced pointedly at the green clock on the wall. "I'm afraid they've all left for the day."

"Then let me into my sister's office. I'd like to see if she left something that might indicate where she is. It's urgent that I reach her."

She shifted, looking agitated as she shut down her computer for the day. "I can't do that, sir. All our scientists' work is highly confidential. Only classified personnel are allowed in the research offices, and then, only with clearance from Dr. Bradford and Seaside Securities."

Adam strode out the door, more frustrated than ever. Denise would never leave town without making sure he had a number to reach her. He started his car and headed toward her house. He'd check it out one more time before he relented and talked to Sarah Cutter.

SARAH CLIMBED from her car, fought with her umbrella which completely turned upside down with the gusty wind, and rushed up the sidewalk to her apartment, ducking her head to dodge the drizzling rain. Water seeped inside her shoes, soaking her feet, and she shivered, a chill engulfing her as she ran up the steps. If only she could get the frightened woman's voice out of her head...

Early spring flowers jutted from window boxes of the downtown Savannah homes and the beautiful historic 1790 bed-and-breakfast across the street, hinting at spring and warm weather around the corner, but Sarah felt a fog of gloom descend upon her. Horns honked, a dog barked, a siren wailed in the distance. The garbled noises around her were loud and frightening, the constant barrage assaulting her from every direction. It was all just too much.

She'd wanted to hear music, laughter, beautiful sounds like the song of the robin or a child singing. But so far, she'd heard a woman's terrified cry, obnoxious traffic noises, thunder and the detectives' laughter, which had been harsh and ugly.

Trembling and fighting a massive headache, she unlocked her door, nearly jumping out of her skin when she heard something scraping behind her. Footsteps. Rain sloshing. Had that reporter followed her home? She whirled around, throwing her broken umbrella in front of her like a weapon, her heart pounding.

Sol. She recognized the scent of his aftershave, the smell of the soap he used. Good heavens, she was so focused on distinguishing the sounds around her she'd forgotten to rely on her other senses.

"You scared me to death," she signed, realizing the sound she'd heard had been his footsteps on the pavement.

"Why are you out by yourself in this weather? My God, Sarah, you just had surgery."

"It's just a little spring shower, Sol. Relax." She waved him inside, smiling slightly at the worry in his eyes. Sol had always been protective. She'd known he wouldn't want her venturing out by herself, but she'd never let her impairment keep her from being independent and she didn't intend to relinquish her freedom now.

Worry furrowed his brow. "You look pale."

"I'm fine." She rubbed at her head again and his eyebrows rose. "Just a headache," she admitted.

He cupped the base of her neck, and rubbed the tight muscle. "Where did you go?" Sol asked. "I've been sitting outside your apartment for an hour waiting on you."

Sarah fixed them some tea and settled on the sofa, bracing herself for her godfather's reaction when she told him where she had been. She wasn't surprised when disapproval and worry flitted across his features, but the anger in his voice unnerved her.

"You shouldn't have gone to the police." Sol paced to the opposite side of the room by the bookcases and studied the family photos on the wall, his shoulders hunched. When he turned to face her, his gray eyes reflected concern, his wrinkles drawn around his mouth. "You had bad dreams, *strange* dreams, when you were little and underwent all those surgeries, Sarah, remember? Some of the dreams were a direct result of the medication, some of them from the trauma you suffered when you were little. Why can't you see that this is the same thing?"

Exhaustion pulled at Sarah, making her signing short and jerky. "I know what I heard. And I think it was real."

"What did the police say?"

She hesitated, picked up her cat, Tigger, and hugged him to her chest. "They didn't believe me."

Sol nodded. "Promise me you'll see Dr. Armstrong—"

"He's a shrink," Sarah protested. "I don't need to

see a shrink." Pain shot through her temple and she swayed on the sofa, but Sol steadied her.

"I think I'd better lie down," Sarah whispered.

Sol nodded and helped her to her room. "Yes, rest now, honey. We'll talk about this later."

After Sol left, Sarah changed into a comfortable blue nightshirt, stretched out, closed her eyes and tried to block out the sounds of the storm raging outside along with the worry in Sol's voice and the sound of the woman's terrified cries. Sol didn't want to believe anything bad had happened at the research center. After all, he was the director and cofounder of CIRP and oversaw the various companies that relocated there. CIRP was still campaigning to draw new companies in. He was the perfect man for the job, but he also knew the sting of negative publicity. After all, Sol had been left to clean up her father's mess.

Still, the woman had sounded so frightened— Sarah had to believe that her cries for help had been real.

ADAM JIMMIED THE LOCK on his sister's back door and crept into her apartment. Not bothering to turn on the lights, he called her name softly, even though he instinctively knew she wasn't home. Four days worth of newspapers lay piled on her front stoop, her mailbox had been crammed full of unopened mail and her indoor plants drooped from lack of care.

The hair on the back of his neck stood on end. His sister was a type A personality. She paid her bills on time, tended to her plants religiously and kept her house neat and orderly. Like clockwork, she read the paper with her morning coffee. He'd lectured her on precautionary measures for a woman living alone ages ago, and she adhered to them rigidly, just as she did the other details in her life. When she traveled, she always asked him to bring in her mail so a possible burglar wouldn't know she'd left town.

Now, although things appeared neat on the surface, the house smelled unoccupied, hinting at her absence. He quickly searched the rooms but found nothing amiss, then checked the bathroom for wet towels but found a lone, dry towel hanging neatly on the chrome bar. Even odder, her makeup was sitting on the vanity. His anxiety growing, he checked the closet in her extra bedroom. Her suitcase was sitting inside, where she always kept it. If she had left town without telling him, why hadn't she packed a suitcase or taken her cosmetics?

He booted up her computer and scrolled her file manager, searching for her calendar, but he needed her password. What would Denise choose as her password?

His palms grew moist as he punched in guesses—her birthday, his birthday, her graduation date. Frustrated, he pounded the machine. What was the biggest day in Denise's life? The day she'd earned her doctorate. Bingo.

Minutes later, he scanned her schedule. She didn't have plans to leave town until July, over three months from now. In fact she had meetings with her research assistant set up this week to discuss her current project, but as usual she had some acronym, a code name, for the project to keep it secret. He'd have to talk to her assistant.

More worried now, he searched the file drawers for notes and found several pads filled with statistics, chemistry and math equations, stuff he didn't begin to understand but knew were important to her work. Denise had also kept a daily journal since she was twelve. He searched her office, but couldn't locate it, so he hurried to the den, but came up empty again. Finally he discovered the thick navy-bound book wedged between her pillows. He hesitated before opening it—this journal was private. Denise never allowed anyone to read it, and had been furious when he'd asked her about it as a teenager. He'd violate her privacy if he read it now.

But what if it told him where she was?

The storm reached a crescendo outside and so had Adam's nerves. Denise never went anywhere without taking her journal. *Never.* She had only been thirteen when their parents died. The journal had been like a security blanket to her, a place to pour out her troubled feelings.

The simple fact that the book was here confirmed his suspicions. Something bad had happened to his sister, and if she had left town, she hadn't left of her own free will.

Chapter Three

Instead of a restful, soothing nap, the voices came to Sarah again. Dull, muffled, breaking in and out, destroying her peace.

"Wh…at are you g…oing to do to me?"

"Just shut u…p, the…"

"No!"

"Re…lax, Doc, it won't…hurt. It'll j…ust sting a little."

Sarah bolted up, sweat-drenched sheets tangled around her legs, her pulse racing, her breath coming in gasps. She had to have been dreaming. How else was it possible for her to hear the same voices in the hospital and here again in her own house? Her house was empty. So where had the voices come from? The doctors had mentioned delayed hearing—was that what was happening? Were these voices a part of the conversation she'd heard in the hospital?

Lightning streaked through the blinds and she fisted the sheets in her hands, fighting her unshakable terror of the storm. Shadows from the starless night hovered about her bedroom, taunting her. Lightning flashed again.

No, not lighting—her apartment lights were blinking signifying someone was at her door. This time a ding sounded in the background.

The doorbell. She'd never heard it before and had assumed when she'd had the apartment customized to fit her needs, they'd disconnected it. Thankfully, the bell emitted a soft musical sound that reminded her of bells ringing, one familiar sound from childhood. She pushed her hair from her face, grabbed a robe and stumbled toward the den, then checked the peephole, expecting to see Sol again. But that big detective, Adam Black, stood on her doorstep, dripping rain from his black hair, his dark face even more intimidating in the shadows with lightning illuminating his hard, sexy features. His eyes were almost as dark as his hair, his cheekbones etched in granite, his shoulders so broad he must have to custom order his clothes. He pounded the door with his fist and she jumped, then finally pulled herself together enough to unlock the door.

"Can I come in?"

She flinched at the harsh set of his jaw as she read his lips. He smelled of rain and wet leather and some earthly scent that reminded her of the woods and sex. Her stomach quivered. Why did the man make her think like that?

He had a black leather jacket slung around his broad shoulders and a pair of well-worn jeans hugged his muscular thighs. Encased in work boots that had seen better days, his feet seemed enormous. He looked as if he should be riding a wild mustang across the prairie.

Or riding a woman in the darkness of her bedroom.

Shaken by her own thoughts, her legs threatened to buckle so she clutched the wall for support.

He seemed oblivious to her reaction. "Look, Miss Cutter, I'm getting soaked. Can I come in?"

A clap of thunder boomed and she jumped, the sound almost as shocking as the tension radiating between them.

He must have realized she was too stunned to move so he pushed his way inside, more gently than she'd imagined, then kicked his boots on the hall rug, brushing his jacket to alleviate the moisture soaking his hair. She stepped inside the kitchen, retrieved a towel and handed it to him. Their hands brushed slightly and heat suffused her, fire curling low in her stomach. His gaze dropped to her cotton robe where it had fallen open at her breasts, revealing the thin nightshirt she'd thrown on to sleep. She belted the robe, a blush rushing up her face. Why did this stranger affect her so? He didn't like her. And she wasn't sure she liked him.

He studied her silently as he ran the towel over his head, down his face and long neck. Finally, he handed the towel back to her, a half smile curving his mouth. "I won't bite, you know."

She felt like a fool and braced herself for his teasing laughter.

But he didn't laugh. Instead he kept watching her with those mesmerizing eyes.

"You got any coffee?"

She stared at him, then signed, "What are you doing here?"

"I don't read sign language," he said.

Resigned, she silently cursed herself for even trying, and reached for her Palm Pilot. "What are you doing here?"

"I need to ask you some more questions."

Fury snaked through her. "To make fun of me again?"

He studied her for a long moment, his dark eyes raking over her, lingering on her mouth. Finally he shook his head. "No. I'm sorry about that. I want to hear your story."

"Why?"

He motioned toward the kitchen and she remembered he'd asked for coffee, so she made a pot, then poured them both a cup, not surprised when he took his black. Her hands trembled when she handed him his mug.

They sat at her small pine table, the room feeling unbearably small with his large body taking up all the space. He seemed to take in the details of her kitchen, the cheery yellow paint and ceramic cats, with a tiny smirk. She tried not to look at his mouth, to wonder what he would look like if those full lips ever really smiled. But even if she hadn't latched on to his mouth to read his lips, she would have been mesmerized by them. He wrapped his big powerful hands around the yellow coffee mug and she decided he had to be the sexiest, most masculine man she'd ever laid eyes on.

Tigger loped in and rubbed up against him, and he surprised her by reaching down and scratching the tabby's back. She couldn't believe her cat had taken to this man. Tigger usually reserved affection for her and her alone. Where was his loyalty?

"Does he go out?"

Sarah shook her head, biting her lip when he frowned at the cat's mangled tail. But if the cat's deformity repulsed him, he didn't show it.

"Okay, tell me once more about this woman you

heard.'' He sipped the coffee, his intense gaze trapping hers.

She hesitated at the spark of awareness in his eyes.

"You said you wanted to help this woman?"

"Why?" she wrote. "Do you believe me now?"

"Maybe. Let's just say I went to the research center and did some checking."

Sarah sat back in the chair, her breath catching. He'd actually followed up and done what she'd asked. Just when she'd convinced herself everything had been a dream, he'd found something to substantiate her story? "I...a..." She hesitated, trying to think how to word her next question. "Is there a Dr. Harden or Harper who works there?"

"Dr. Harley."

Oh, God. "And she's missing?"

Pain darkened his black eyes, the first real emotion she'd seen, other than that simmering sexuality. "I have reason to believe she is."

Her pulse raced. "Who is she?"

He ran a hand through his hair, raised his head and looked straight into her eyes, a sense of desolation radiating from him. "My sister."

Adam steeled himself against the sympathy in Sarah Cutter's cornflower-blue eyes, and the allure of knowing she was half-naked beneath that flimsy robe as he explained briefly about Denise's sudden vacation.

"Write down everything you remember," he said gruffly. He sipped his coffee, once again zeroing in on the faint scars on her hands as she wrote.

Basically, her story remained the same as before, offering him little to go on. As had Denise's journal. He had a few more pages to skim, but so far the portions described very personal feelings about her divorce and her co-workers, with a few notations about apprehension over her research.

"Are you sure you didn't hear someone mention her name before your surgery, then you dreamed about her afterward?"

"I couldn't hear before the surgery."

"But you read lips, right?"

She nodded.

"You might have seen her name on a chart somewhere?"

Her writing became short and jerky. "I didn't hear anyone mention her name before the surgery and I don't remember seeing her name anywhere, either. Does she work with hearing implants?"

"No, neurology. Tell me about the implants. You said they were a special prototype?"

"Yes, they're still in the experimental stages. I had several surgeries when I was young, but there was too much damage to my ear to repair. This implant has a special microchip inside. It's similar, but even more sophisticated than the cochlear implants and another new one that's under clinical study called the Vibrant Soundbridge."

"What are those two?"

"With the Vibrant Soundbridge, an electronic receiver is implanted behind the ear. A wire leads down to an electromagnet that's attached to one of the middle ear bones. The brain interprets the vibrations as sound. The cochlear ones are electronic systems that send sound-generated impulses directly to the cochlea. Mine is surgically implanted and not visible like most hearing aids." She paused and glanced at him, and he urged her to continue. "My father worked on the project years ago, but they didn't have the technology to make it successful. When the Coastal Island Research Park opened the center on Catcall, the project was revamped. I'm the first person to receive this implant. It's still in the clinical trial stages."

He let that information sink in. Could there be some element of the hearing implant that allowed her to pick up sounds far away? "If your hearing is more acute, why aren't you being bombarded by constant noises and voices?"

"I am, but it's sporadic. The doctor said there may be some residual sounds, even a delayed reaction. Like a stroke patient, my nerves and brain have to learn to work together again."

He frowned. "What else did you hear? Did my sister call this man's name?"

She shook her head.

"Did you hear any sounds in the background? Anybody else in the room?"

She pressed her fingers to her temple in thought—either that or she had a headache—then answered no.

"Did he say where he was taking her?"

"No."

He cursed in frustration and saw her flinch, then forced himself to ask the question he'd been avoiding. "Did he say what he planned to do to her?"

Emotions etched themselves on her face. She'd been affected by the woman's cries, he realized, then found himself wondering why he believed her now when earlier he'd thought she was a kook. He wished to hell she'd talk, too, instead of scribbling on that damned computer.

Just once he wanted to hear her voice, to see if it

sounded low and sexy or if she'd speak in a soft purr or…

He shook the thoughts away, focusing on her writing.

"He didn't say exactly, only that she should shut up or he would kill her. But…" she hesitated, watched his reaction, as if she were trying to decide whether or not to reveal the details of the woman's attack.

"Look, don't hold anything back. If this man has my sister, time might be running out."

Her gaze remained glued to his mouth as if she were reading his lips, then she wrote, "When I heard them in the hospital, I thought he knocked her unconscious because I heard a thud as if she'd fallen to the floor."

"Meaning the man might have already killed her."

"I don't think so, I heard her moan. Then they argued later."

"You went back to the hospital?"

"No, I heard them—" she hesitated again "—here at home."

Was she telling the truth? How was it possible?

She'd read the questions in his eyes. "I was trying to sleep, but I had a bad headache. The rain, the sirens, it's too much." She frowned. "Probably the delayed hearing the doctor mentioned. The voices I heard here must have been part of the conversation I overheard at the hospital and I'm just now remembering it."

He waited, his teeth gritted. "What else?"

"She was begging him not to hurt her. He warned her she'd feel a slight sting, she cried out, then everything went quiet again."

"He drugged her." The realization sickened Adam, but at least maybe Denise was still alive. But why would someone kidnap and drug her?

The possibilities raced through his mind. A jealous co-worker at the research center? Her husband who'd been bitter about the separation? Or worse, a stranger who'd been stalking her and planned to do God knew what?

AN HOUR LATER, Sarah collapsed with exhaustion, praying the detective would find his sister and that she wouldn't hear the voices again. She couldn't stand the pain in the woman's cries.

Then again, if she didn't hear the woman's voice, she wouldn't be able to help her. And she had never backed down from anything in her life. She couldn't let her fears keep her a prisoner.

She stared at the card the detective had left on the table with his phone number. Without even knowing Adam Black, he pulled at feelings so dormant she thought they'd died completely after her disastrous relationship with her old boyfriend, Kevin.

Maybe she was afraid, she admitted silently, but she didn't want to see Detective Black again. His eyes and body blazed with anger and attitude, the kind of cold, harsh facade that would hold any woman at arm's length. He was in control and would want to control everyone around him, especially someone he considered weaker. Someone with a handicap.

But he obviously loved his sister.

She hoped he found her before it was too late.

Determined to banish him from her mind, she turned her thoughts to her normal life. To the school for the deaf where she'd been teaching. Pulling out her plan book, she checked the plans she'd penciled in for the substitute teacher. Her class would take a hike tomorrow to collect items for a nature collage. Then they'd watch a film about the seasons and the rebirth spring promised. Just as she thought she'd have a rebirth when she'd regained her hearing. She'd taken a six-week leave of absence following her surgery to recover and acclimate herself to living in a hearing world.

Now, for some odd reason, she found herself wanting to return to the safety of the silent world she'd always lived in. Back to her teaching job at the school, to her co-workers, who communicated the way she did—with sign language. Back to the safety of knowing she didn't have to interact with dangerous, sexy men like Adam Black.

Men who made her want to be whole again.

Chapter Four

Adam spent a restless night trying to forget the magnetic pull between him and Sarah Cutter. He couldn't pinpoint it, but something about the woman unleashed his baser instincts. She was troubled, confused and just about the most needy woman he'd ever met.

Yet, he was the one who felt needy in her presence. As if he might shrivel up if he didn't touch her. He didn't like the feeling. Adam Black was a loner. He took care of himself and his sister; he didn't need anyone else.

Hell, when had he last woken up in a sweat from wanting a woman? A long damn time.

Because he'd learned the hard way. The last time he had gotten involved with a woman, a *witness,* named Pamela, the end had been disastrous. He'd been too distracted by her to focus on his job, and it had cost her her life.

Now his job, staying in control, was everything—it had to be.

Determined to squash the emotions churning through him, he took a cold shower and dressed. When he'd arrived home the night before, he'd tried to contact Denise's research assistant, but supposedly the man's grandmother had died and he'd flown to Los Angeles for the funeral. Adam had stayed up half the night researching hearing implants on the Internet, looking at the latest developments in technology. But he found nothing on a device that might allow a person to hear through walls or serve as a transmitter.

Clayton met him at the station. "Uh-oh, Black, you're not going to like this."

Adam stared in shock at the headliner on a local tabloid, his mind reeling as he read the article.

Hearing Things?

Cold War spy's daughter who has been deaf for twenty years claims to have heard evidence of a kidnapping, possible murder!

Sarah Cutter ended twenty years of silence four days ago when she received surgically implanted hearing aids by doctors at the research center on Catcall Island, the new facility which has been linked with the government-owned buildings on Nighthawk Island.

Late Thursday afternoon, she rushed to the police claiming that while she was in the hospital she overheard a woman being abducted....

The article continued to describe what Sarah had told him, then launched into an account of how she'd lost her hearing.

Twenty years ago, five-year-old Sarah lost her hearing in the explosion that killed both her parents. Her father, Dr. Charles Cutter, a scientist and former Navy lieutenant, had been working on a secret project for the government developing a listening device to be used in the Cold War. Cutter's technology died with his death. Evidence later verified that Cutter had made a deal to sell the device to the Russians. Reports confirmed that Cutter's own wife discovered his intentions and had planned to turn him over to the government. When Cutter realized his wife's plans, he set fire to their house, but was accidentally caught in the explosion and killed as well. Some speculate he might have killed himself to avoid facing a court-martial and prison sentence. A close friend and one of Cutter's co-workers, Sol Santenelli, arrived just in time to rescue the five-year-old child from the burning home. Dr. Santenelli is now the director of the CIRP, Coastal Island Research Park.

Although Sarah underwent stringent psychological evaluations, as well as several surgeries which were unsuccessful in repairing her hearing loss, she never spoke afterward. Cutter was buried with a dishonorable discharge.

Adam scrubbed his hand across his face.

Why hadn't Sarah told him about her past? Did she know exactly what her father had been working on? Of course, the CIA and FBI had sophisticated listening devices now, but twenty years ago the technology would have been cutting edge and worth a small fortune.

Clayton whistled. "Pretty interesting, huh?"

"Yeah. But why the hell did Sarah Cutter go to the tabloids with the story?"

"Maybe she wanted the attention. She might have

made up the whole story just to get her name in the paper.''

Clayton might be right. The story didn't exactly paint a picture of a healthy emotional female.

Then again, he'd seen the fear on her face when she'd described the kidnapping. Growing up with a handicap, she had to have faced ridicule before. Yet, she'd come to them with the bizarre story knowing they would laugh at her. Either she was lying or she had a great deal of courage.

He knew that kind of courage. And he had to admire it.

He had to talk to her again. Crazy or not, attraction or not, she might be the key to finding his sister.

But *if* there was any truth to Sarah's story, printing her name in the papers had put her in danger.

SARAH HUGGED each of the children in her class, grateful to spend the afternoon with some sense of normalcy.

"Is it fun to be able to hear?" five-year-old Jason signed.

"What does music sound like?" curly-haired Claire asked.

Betty Ann clapped her hands. "And the choo-choo train? I always wanted to hear a train whistle!"

Sarah waved for them all to pay attention and signed, "My hearing isn't perfect yet, so I don't understand all the sounds around me. I feel like a kindergartner again, having to recognize certain sounds and name them."

The kids giggled.

"Some sounds are lovely, but some are harsh and

loud, like the horns honking and bulldozers. The fire engine and ambulance siren is loud and screechy and sends a chill up my back.''

The children's eyes widened in awe as she elaborated, many of them unable to imagine what the word *sound* truly meant. They had been taught that vibrations produced sound, but learning about them and experiencing them were two different things, especially for the children born totally deaf or with a profound hearing loss.

''I can't distinguish tones yet so I still haven't been able to enjoy music, but the doctors say my hearing should improve daily.''

''Will you come back?'' Jason asked.

''Yes, soon.'' Sarah hugged each of them again, then turned to the director of the center, Adrianne Waters. ''I miss everyone so much.''

''Are you adapting to life in the hearing world?'' Adrianne asked.

Sarah forced a stiff smile and signed, ''Yes. Take care of my babies here.''

Adrianne laughed, the first beautiful sound Sarah had heard. Adrianne had suffered her hearing loss when she was a teen, so her language skills were advanced. Maybe she could help Sarah with her speech.

When she was ready.

And maybe Adrianne would be the next volunteer for a hearing implant.

Right now, Sarah simply wanted to go home and lie down. The twinge of a headache wore at her, as did a slight ringing in her ears. Exhaustion crept up on her, too, from her sleepless night. For hours she'd lain awake, waiting for the voices, hoping they wouldn't come, then hoping they would so she'd know Denise Harley was still alive.

So she'd have good news to tell Adam Black.

ADAM HAD BEEN pacing on Sarah's front stoop for thirty minutes. He'd finally convinced himself to leave when he saw her walking down the sidewalk. She looked pale and tired, but she was alive and safe. He breathed a sigh of relief. Worry had dogged him all afternoon. At the same time, anger made him want to shake her.

Her steps faltered momentarily when she spotted him, then she raised her chin and strode toward him. He shoved his hands in his pockets, resisting the urge to touch her. She looked so damn vulnerable and sexy that his groin tightened. The soft fabric of her dress clung to her subtle curves and that long dark hair was blowing in the breeze, giving him a glimpse of the sultry line of her neck. Once again that magnetic draw between them heated up. He wanted to hold her, just once. To hear her voice.

But he wouldn't.

She faced him with raised brows as if to ask why he'd come.

"We have to talk."

She nodded curtly, unlocked her door and started to step inside, but he pressed a gentle hand on her back to still her and stepped inside first. He glanced around, his breath easing out when he found everything in order.

She frowned at him, as if she had no idea why he'd go into her apartment first. But old habits were hard to break, and his cop instincts made him suspicious. And cautious.

She led him to the kitchen and brewed a pot of coffee. But he didn't want coffee. He wanted answers.

He slapped the paper on the table. "What's this all about?"

She startled at the sound of his sharp voice and glanced at the table. But her face paled when she read the headline.

She didn't know about the article?

Her gaze rose to his, shadows haunting her eyes as she toyed with the necklace again. He wondered what significance the locket had, whether she had pictures inside?

He crossed his arms, determined not to be distracted by her vulnerability or the sizzle of attraction between them.

"Did you talk to that scumbag?" Adam asked.

She shook her head no. Then with trembling fingers, she picked up the paper and began to read.

SARAH COULDN'T believe this was happening.

Baring It All— Hearing Things?

Dear heavens.

She scanned the article, her stomach growing queasy. The reporter had lied to her—he didn't work for the *Savannah Times*. He worked for a sleazy tabloid. And he'd printed her life story in the paper for everyone to read. She twisted the chain around her neck, thinking of the picture of her mother inside. Once it had held a photo of her father, as well.

But she'd taken it out when she'd learned the truth about him.

How had the reporter gotten this story? And why dredge up things that had happened twenty years ago?

Her mind raced back to the police station. He must

have seen the note she'd written to the detectives. Had they shown it to him?

No, Detective Black obviously hadn't. She skimmed the last paragraph and her legs buckled. Robey Burgess made her sound like a lunatic. Sol would be furious. Shaken, she sank into the chair and met Adam's gaze.

Obviously, he thought she'd sold her story just to see her name in the headlines.

"Did you give him the story?"

She shook her head again and mouthed the word *no*.

The detective moved toward her. He surprised her by reaching out with one big thumb and slowly wiping a tear from her cheek. "Did you talk to him at all?"

She inhaled sharply, fighting the strong need to hold on to him. "He followed me to the car after I left the police station, but I told him to leave me alone," she wrote on a piece of paper.

"That was the reason you raced out of the parking lot?"

She nodded and started to scribble an explanation, but her hands were shaking so badly she dropped the pen and it rolled across the floor.

He sat down beside her, then shocked her by pulling her hands into his larger ones. His touch felt amazingly gentle. His dark eyes watched her, caressing her with a kind of tenderness she hadn't expected, causing a slow ache to burn in her belly. How long had it been since a man had touched her? Had looked at her in any way except pity?

How long had it been since a man had wanted her?

But what would a strong, tough man like Adam Black see in a woman like her?

"I have to warn you, Sarah," he said in a low voice. "I don't know exactly what's going on here, but if you did hear something about my sister, the fact that the story was printed could put you in danger."

"LOOK, SOL, I didn't talk to the reporter. In fact I refused to," Sarah signed in frustration. As if the meeting with Adam hadn't left her rattled enough, Sol had arrived on her doorstep the moment Adam had driven away. She couldn't believe she'd actually mistaken the detective's concern for her, his interest in the information she had, as interest in her personally. She was a fool. He'd told her to be careful, to call if she remembered anything else. Then he'd left her place like a man on a foxhunt, and for some odd reason, she'd felt very alone.

"Sarah?"

Sol's voice pulled her back to the moment. "He followed me and talked to someone at the police department," she signed, not wanting to tell him about the note, "or maybe he eavesdropped."

"I'm suing the little bastard! He'll never work in this goddamn city again!"

Sarah's hands released the death grip she held on her coffee cup to sign, "I'm sorry, Sol. I really am."

He paced the length of her den, pausing to look at her mother's photo. "I promised Charles I'd take care of you when you were christened. Part of that is keeping his name out of the paper. I hate the way the country crucified him back then. All that Cutter's Crossing garbage."

"So do I. And I certainly don't want all that history dragged up again."

"It looks as if this sleazeball intended to do just that. I've already got a call in to my lawyer." He tunneled his hands through his thinning hair, pacing across the room. "Just think what this negative publicity might mean for the research center, Sarah. Arnold Hughes and I are just now getting CIRP off the ground. Catcall's not even filled to capacity, and we still have a lot of space on Whistlestop to fill. I intend to make CIRP the research mecca of the world."

Sarah signed, "I said I was sorry, Sol. Besides the article made *me* look crazy—it didn't reflect badly on the center."

Sol took her by the shoulders. "Promise me you won't talk to any reporters or the police again. This mess has to die down, Sarah."

Sarah tensed in his tight grip.

He frowned, then released her and gathered his jacket. "I have to meet Hughes. We're having a press conference to deal with this situation before it snowballs out of control."

Sarah bit her lip, thinking about Detective Black and his sister.

"Sarah? Promise me. You don't want the center to get shut down, do you?"

"No, of course not." Sarah wrapped her arms around her middle. She owed her life to Sol. His whole life revolved around the center.

She'd never do anything to hurt him or CIRP.

FROM WHERE HE STOOD at the reception desk, Adam heard the two doctors in the back arguing. Miss Johnson's nervous gaze flitted to the door. "Dr. Tucker said he's not available right now."

The voices came again. "This is a damn nightmare!"

"Don't you think I know it? Sarah Cutter's a nutcase!"

Adam arched a brow and said, "Is Dr. Bradford available?"

The receptionist shook her head and reached behind her to shut the door between her cubicle and the main hallway.

The voices cut through the wood. "What the hell was Sarah Cutter thinking? For God's sake, we give her back her hearing and then she spreads some cockamamy story like that to the papers to discredit our center?"

"I've called a press conference for some damage control."

Adam flattened his hands on the desk. "Look, Miss Johnson, I'm not going away until I speak with one of the doctors who worked with my sister."

"I've explained to you that's just not possible." She gestured toward a red button on the side of her desk. "Now if you don't leave, Detective, I'll have to call Security."

"Listen here, miss, if you don't let me talk to Dr. Bradford, I'll haul your skinny little butt in for interfering with an official police investigation." He intentionally leered at her perfectly manicured nails. "And I don't think you'd like some of the women in lockup."

Fear danced in her eyes but she closed her smart mouth, jumped up and ran to the back, her heels clicking on the linoleum floor. He tapped his boot while he waited, deciding to give the doctor three minutes before he jumped over the security line and tore into him.

Two minutes, twenty-five seconds later, Bradford appeared and ushered him into his office. While Bradford cleared stacks of research material from a chair for Adam to sit in, Adam studied the man. He was

Caucasian, short, gray-haired and portly. He wore a lab coat and gray slacks and had narrow, gray eyes with dark circles marring his leathery skin. "Miss Johnson said you were insistent on seeing me."

Adam took the chair while Bradford seated himself behind his desk. "Yes, I want to know where my sister is."

"Your sister?"

"Dr. Denise Harley."

Bradford swallowed, his Adam's apple bobbing up and down. "Your sister's on leave—"

"That's bull." He stood, moving quickly, and jerked Bradford by the collar. "Denise always lets me know where she's going. She wouldn't leave her place without having someone take care of things, and I saw the papers piled on her porch yesterday."

"Maybe she needed time away from her bully brother."

Adam tightened his fingers around the doctor's collar, grinning when the man yelped. "I don't think so." His eyes shot to the tabloid paper lying on the desk, looking oddly out of sorts with the research papers and medical journals.

"That's what this is about, isn't it?" Bradford chuckled without humor. "You're questioning me because of some slimy tabloid reporter's lies? You know those stories are fabrications, pure sensationalistic garbage."

"Except this one may have a seed of truth."

"You talked to that Cutter woman, didn't you? You don't actually believe her?"

Adam's jaw snapped. "I'm checking out her story."

"This is unreal! We help the poor woman restore

her hearing and she invents some wild story to slander us!''

Adam watched a muscle jump in the man's jaw. "She doesn't seem the vindictive type."

"She's confused, Detective. She just had surgery. Did she tell you the possible problems with the implant?'' He described the lack of clarity of sounds, the static breaks, the trouble her brain might have processing the information she heard. "In short, she could have misinterpreted something she'd heard and confused it with dreams. And frankly, I'm not sure she's stable. Just look at her past.''

Adam gritted his teeth at the implication. "I want to see Denise's office."

Bradford shook his head. "I can't let you in there. All research is confidential."

"The hell with confidential! Don't you get it? My sister's missing!''

"That's what you say. I believe she's on vacation as she told me. Therefore, I have no reason to even consider authorizing your request.''

"Because you're hiding something."

"No." Bradford pulled Adam's hand away, then straightened his lab coat. "Because you're chasing something that isn't there, and I'm protecting valuable research.''

Adam realized they'd reached a standstill. He'd have to get a warrant and come back. But he wouldn't give up until he found some answers. He carried enough guilt over Pamela's death.

He had to do everything he could to find Denise. And to protect Sarah.

A FEW MINUTES LATER, Adam stared in shock at his sister's apartment. The place had been ransacked.

Just yesterday it had been neat as a pin, but today magazines and clothes and papers littered the floor as if a tornado had swept through, overturning furniture and creating havoc.

What had the intruder been looking for?

He catalogued the details himself before dialing for a crime team, grimacing at the way the intruder had smeared ketchup and food all over the kitchen. Whoever had done it had wanted them to believe they were vandals.

But Denise's desk had been torn apart, the computer discs were out of place—petty thieves and kids could care less about office files. Although the intruder pilfered her jewelry box, they hadn't stolen the stereo and TV, so the motive hadn't been robbery. Of course, someone could have driven by and scared off the culprit before he'd stolen everything he wanted. Or he might have used robbery as a cover-up for something else.

Denise's estranged husband, Russell, a marine biologist at the center, had been bitter when she'd filed for divorce. Would he do such a thing for revenge? Did she have a boyfriend? No, Denise wouldn't date before her divorce was final. Besides, she was a workaholic, and a social life was the last on her list of priorities.

Women were such targets—anyone could have developed a fixation on her and kidnapped her for their own devious means. Sarah Cutter's porcelain face flashed in his mind; she was so vulnerable.

But Denise was the one in trouble. And her coworkers weren't talking. He had to force them into giving him some answers. A knot of anxiety tightened his chest as Sarah's face flashed in his mind again. If she was the link to finding Denise, and whoever had

Denise knew she'd been helping him, they might go after Sarah.

He'd wait until the crime team arrived and conducted a thorough investigation, then he'd check on Sarah.

A SCREECHING SOUND suddenly jarred Sarah from the first peaceful sleep she'd had in days. She rolled to her back and tried to discern the sound. Tigger sharpening his claws on a cabinet door? The toilet flushing in the apartment next to her? A car's tires protesting on the road in front of her house? The woman, Denise Harley, waking from the drugs?

The screech echoed again. Faint but shrill. A click. Another sound...soft, padding, a squeak—the loose wood board in the apartment. Tigger must be running through the hall. She closed her eyes to focus again as a dull throbbing settled in her ear.

No, the sound was footsteps. The screech the window opening.

Or was her hearing delayed again?

No, the footsteps padded closer. Someone was in her apartment. The door creaked open.

Panicking, she rolled out of bed and reached for the phone. She had to call Detective Black.

But the shadow moved closer. She tried to run, but suddenly the intruder lunged at her, yanking her backward so hard her head hit the corner of the nightstand.

Chapter Five

Sarah tried to scream, but the sound died in her throat. The man fell on top of her, his hands clamped around her neck, squeezing, choking the life out of her. She struggled, clawing at his hands, bucking her body upward to throw him off, but his weight pinned her. He smelled like cigarettes and leather and cheap cologne. But darkness clouded her vision and shadows clung to his ski mask, so she couldn't see his face. Only his black evil eyes leered back at her.

She had to make some noise. She tried to scream again, but her voice died, so she banged her feet on the carpet.

His fingers dug into her throat. Tight. Tighter. She couldn't breathe. She kicked and clawed at his back, but his hands cut off her air. Finally, her arms flopped down beside her and her body went limp.

ADAM'S HEART POUNDED as he careened around the corner to Sarah's town house. The tires squealed as he swerved to avoid a Mazda flying around the corner. The stoplight turned red, but he raced through it, took the corner at fifty, then soared into a parking spot on the street and jumped out. A stray cat screeched and darted across the side alley. He jogged past the two cars nearest Sarah's town house, then crossed the lawn and flew up the steps, his pulse hammering when he noticed the darkened interior. He slammed his hand on the doorbell, heard the ring, saw lights flicker on and off. His breath collected in his lungs as he waited. Nothing. He hit the doorbell again and again, thumping his foot. Still nothing.

Tigger meowed at his feet, sending his nerves on alert. The cat never went out. So why was he out now?

His anxiety growing, he leaned his ear against the door. Silence met him.

Was Sarah at home? If so, why wasn't Tigger inside with her?

A crashing sound broke through the silence. Distant, as if it had come from upstairs. A lamp breaking maybe.

His instincts told him to hurry.

He jimmied the lock and slammed his body against the door. One, two, three times. The door swung open.

Adam's pulse raced as he pulled his gun from his holster and paused in the doorway. The faint scent of cigarette smoke drifted toward him. Scuffling sounds followed. Someone was upstairs.

Tigger darted inside. Adam clenched the automatic in his hands, then crept up the steps, wincing when the old wooden boards creaked.

A wailing sound trilled from above.

He ran up the remaining stairs toward the sound. The first room, a bedroom-turned-study, was empty. A dim light glowed from the back room, maybe a bathroom. He moved on silent feet to the next bedroom, hesitated at the door again, counted to three, then shoved open the door.

"Police, freeze."

Poised with his gun in the firing position, he searched the dark room with his eyes. Shadows claimed the corners and bed and an open curtain fluttered with the breeze. Whoever had been there had just escaped.

He raced to the window, but a blur of dark clothing streaked around the alley. Then a high-pitched wailing sound cut through the air, coming from the other side of the bed.

Sarah.

He crossed the room, and circled to the other side of the bed. A lamp had crashed to the floor, broken glass dotting the gray carpet. Sarah lay curled into a ball on the floor amidst a tangle of sheets and a flimsy white nightgown, her hands stroking her throat as she gasped for air.

SARAH ROCKED herself back and forth, her throat aching as she dragged oxygen into her lungs. As if she'd floated into unconsciousness, then was drifting back, she realized the man had released her. Where had he gone?

Suddenly he grabbed her again, pulling her upward. His strong hands clamped around her arms, and she flung her fists at him, pelting his chest, crying out wildly.

"Shh, it's me, Sarah, Adam Black." He gripped her chin and angled her head so she had to look at his face. "Stop fighting me, I'm here to help."

Through the haze of panic, his words finally registered. His dark hair, the nearly black eyes, that small cleft in his chin. She stared at him helplessly, but dropped her hands, giving up the fight. Her body sagged against him as his strong arms embraced her.

"You're all right now," he said in a gruff voice. "I've got you, sweetheart."

A deep trembling started inside her, invading every nerve in her body. She wanted to nod, to tell him she was fine, but she opened her mouth and a careening sound erupted that sounded foreign and ghastly to her own ears.

He cupped her face in his hands. "Shh, take a deep breath. Now another." His voice sounded oddly gentle and soothing compared to the menacing look on his face that tears sprang to her eyes and seeped down her cheeks. She hated to cry. He brushed the tears away with the pad of his thumb, then gently traced the bruises on her neck.

His voice was low again, his thick eyebrows narrowed. "Did he hurt you anywhere else?"

Though the fog of panic had receded slightly, she still had trouble understanding him. His voice cracked, the sounds delayed slightly as she tried to decipher them.

His hands skated over her body, checking for injuries. "Sarah, tell me you're all right."

The fear in his voice finally registered, and she mouthed the words, "I'm okay."

He traced the small knot where she'd hit her head on the night table. "You are hurt. We have to have the paramedics check you out. Are you dizzy? Nauseous?"

She shook her head no, pressing her hand to her mouth as another sob built inside.

"It's okay," Adam whispered roughly. "Go ahead

and let it out.'' His own chest heaving, he pulled her into his arms and held her, murmuring comforting words as he gently stroked her back. His fingers found their way to her hair, and he tenderly tucked it behind her ear, one hand combing down the tangled strands. Painful memories bombarded her, but she struggled to hold her cries inside. The fear she'd felt when the man had broken in surged through her again, the terror when she thought she was about to die. Flashes of the explosion when she was five followed. She hated being vulnerable, clinging to this man as if she were afraid to let go, but she couldn't bear to pull away, not just yet. She felt too safe in his arms.

"I was scared to death when I heard the scuffling," he murmured near her ear. "I just came from Denise's. Her apartment was ransacked, and I was afraid—" he paused, stroking her cheek with his finger "—I was afraid whoever had done it would come after you."

With trembling fingers, she raised her hand along his jaw. She saw the fear in his eyes for his sister, the worry, but also concern for her. Heat radiated from his taut muscles, and his masculine scent filled her nostrils, igniting her senses.

His heart beat thunderously against the palm of her hand. For a second, emotions warred within his eyes as he searched her face. Then his gaze dropped to her mouth and heat flared in his eyes. With a low growl in his throat, he lowered his head, brushed his lips across hers and kissed her.

Sarah tasted like cinnamon tea and salty tears and sweetness. Adam couldn't resist sweeping his tongue across her lips, then delving inside to taste her. She clung to him, her fine-boned hands gently holding on to the corded muscles of his arms, her soft whispery breath floating over his mouth. Heat spread through him, sending a surge of desire straight to his sex.

He willed himself to pull away.

Instead, one hand snaked through her hair while the other dragged her to him, pressing her delicate curves into the hard plains of his body. They fit perfectly, he realized, her supple breasts rising and falling rapidly as he deepened the kiss.

But Sarah had just been assaulted, he reasoned, his common sense finally overriding his baser instincts. And he was here as a cop, not as a boyfriend or lover.

What the hell was he doing?

Regret and disgust washed over him, and he slowly pulled away, well aware his body's reaction had not been subtle. His breathing sounded raspy in the thick silence that hung between them, his desire to repeat the mistake so strong, he had to lower his hands to his side to keep from kissing her.

She looked dazed as she moved away from him, but not afraid, as he expected, and not terrified as she had been when he'd found her curled on the floor. At least he'd taken that horrible fear from her vibrant blue eyes for a few seconds.

"I'm sorry," he muttered, unable to express himself any better.

She shook her head as if to tell him he needn't apologize.

Had she wanted the kiss, or had the situation simply called for comfort from whoever was available?

It didn't matter. Hell, he had a case to think of. A job to do.

A sister to find.

And he had to protect Sarah because she might be

the key to finding Denise. He couldn't get personally involved with her, though; she was way too complicated.

Memories of Pamela—the witness he'd slept with, the one who'd gotten killed in the crossfire when their safe house location had been discovered— rode into his head, reminding him of a dozen different reasons why he shouldn't touch Sarah Cutter.

"I…" He jammed his hands in his pockets. "Are you all right?"

She nodded, smoothing her wrinkled gown with shaky hands. His gaze dropped to the thin cotton of the garment, the pale moonlight haloing her face and the curves of her body that lay beneath. The curves that had ignited his hunger only a few moments before. The curves that had felt delicious in his hands.

Shame filled him. His big hands could crush her if he wasn't careful. She was vulnerable and he'd taken advantage of her frightened state.

She grabbed a thick velour robe from the bed, slipped it on and quickly knotted it. He spotted her locket on the floor and picked it up, then handed it to her. She clutched it in her fingers, then pressed it to her chest.

"Did you recognize the man who attacked you?"

Sarah shook her head.

"Did anything about him seem familiar?"

Again, she answered with a shake of her head.

"I need to call this in." He dragged his gaze away from her to reach for the phone. "I'll have the lab fingerprint your place in case we catch the guy's prints. And I'll get a paramedic to check you out."

She nodded, that frail look crossing her face again as she glanced at the broken lamp on the floor.

Still, Adam couldn't shake the strange connection he'd had with Sarah when they'd kissed. Or the fact that she hadn't pushed him away when she should have.

A HALF HOUR LATER, the paramedic concluded Sarah had a slight concussion, but she would be fine. He cautioned her to call her specialist if she noticed any significant changes in her hearing ability or residual pain from the blow to her head. Sarah described her assault via her Palm Pilot, while other detectives dusted her place for fingerprints. The evening finally seemed to be coming to an end. Reliving the experience as she'd described it to the police had been difficult. So had trying to forget that heated kiss with Adam Black.

Sarah had never felt so exposed, so in danger, yet so safe at the same time.

But Adam had reverted to being the detective again—he'd avoided any personal contact with her for the duration of the questions, and when he had spoken to her, he wore a mask of professionalism. Occasionally, she'd glimpsed the regret in his eyes, as if he wished he'd never touched her. As if he were sorry he might have given her the wrong idea.

She'd seen that one kind of regret before, from other men.

They'd be attracted to her at first, at least physically. A few had thought her handicap intriguing, even challenging, for a while. Then reality settled in, an embarrassing situation arose where they had trouble communicating, and their relationship ended. But none of the other men had been half as sexy and masculine as Adam.

The reason she'd probably reacted to him so intensely.

She had to forget about him, other than as her protector.

He walked his partner, Clayton Fox, to the door and they spoke in hushed voices before he finally turned to her. She cradled a cup of tea in her still-shaky hands, sipping it slowly as if the warm liquid could calm her.

He moved like a lion, his stride long and purposeful, his expression stony as he took the overstuffed armchair opposite her. Splaying his hands on his thighs, he leaned forward. "I'll stay the night," he said in a gruff voice.

Sarah nearly dropped the saucer. It clattered in her hands as she swung her gaze to the detective. Her lips parted involuntarily to mouth the word, "What?"

A muscle ticked in his jaw. "I said I'll stay tonight."

She shook her head, her mind racing.

"In case this creep comes back."

She grabbed the Palm Pilot and wrote, "No."

He arched one dark brow. "Look, Sarah, you may think this was a random burglar, but I don't. Think about it. The tabloid story about you overhearing a kidnapping, my sister's ransacked place, your attacks, they all occurred in the same day." He blew out a breath. "Too coincidental for me."

Fear seeped back inside her, chilling her to the bone. "But you don't need to stay—"

He pressed his fingers against her hand and her gaze swung back to his. "If you're worried about me, don't. I won't touch you again."

The harsh tone to his voice rode on already frayed

nerves. He obviously saw her imperfections, her lack of experience, and deemed her not a whole woman because of them.

"We can assign another officer to protect you if you'd rather. I'll arrange better security on your place tomorrow." He raked a hand through his thick black hair. "But I still need to talk to you about my sister."

"All right," she wrote. "But you don't need to stay here tonight. I'll go to my godfather's."

He studied her for a long moment. "Where does he live?"

"He owns an estate on Catcall Island."

Both his brows rose. "It's secure?"

Sarah nodded. "He's one of the founders of the research center, CIRP. Seaside Securities provides security for him as well as for the center."

Adam stood. "All right. Pack a bag. I'll drive you over."

Sarah shook her head to argue, but he caught her arm.

"Look, you don't have to be afraid of me, Sarah." He cleared his throat. "I was out of line earlier, but I told you it won't happen again. I will keep you safe."

Sarah's heart fluttered. He'd keep her safe from danger, but who would protect her from him?

THE FIFTEEN-MINUTE RIDE from Savannah to Catcall Island dragged by, fraught with tension. Adam suggested phoning Sarah's godfather before they drove over, but she'd refused, saying she didn't want to alarm him.

The man had a right to be alarmed.

If her godfather loved her half as much as she claimed he did, he'd hire a bodyguard for her himself.

Sarah wrestled with her hands in her lap, twisting them around the denim skirt she'd changed into when she'd packed an overnight bag. Even though Adam had turned on the radio, the soft jazz music couldn't dissolve the tension.

She rested her head against the seat and closed her eyes. The contours of her pale skin glowed in the moonlight, the stark bruises on her neck a glaring reminder of the attack. Could she help him find Denise? But how? She didn't know the kidnapper's identity or where they'd taken Denise. Her vague information wouldn't be worth killing over.

Unless…unless he was wrong and the attack wasn't related to his sister's disappearance. But why else would someone want her dead?

"Sarah, are you involved with anyone right now?"

An odd look crossed her face and he realized she might have misunderstood him.

"I'm just wondering if you had a jealous boyfriend, maybe one who got angry when you broke up and might want to retaliate."

She shook her head no. Shadows haunted her eyes, making him wonder if he'd touched a nerve. She'd also put her necklace back on and worried the end with her fingers.

"Other than the connection with Denise, can you think of anyone or any other reason someone else would want to hurt you?"

Frown lines creased her forehead, but she shook her head no again.

The sound of a ship's foghorn in the distance

brought her head up. Her button nose wrinkled as she tried to discern the sound.

"It's a foghorn," he said, unable to keep a small smile from his mouth.

Her lips parted in response, and his gut clenched. In some ways she was like a child discovering the world. Yet she still couldn't speak, or verbalize her needs without the aid of that Palm Pilot or pen and paper.

She gestured toward a sign and he turned onto the street leading to her godfather's estate. Within seconds, they'd passed two of the newer developments on the island and faced the security gate at her godfather's.

Opulent was the only way to describe the ten-acre estate where Sol Santenelli resided. Another reminder of the difference between Sarah and himself, Adam thought. An Italian villa-style structure with wrought-iron fences sat on sprawling green grass, a front garden area, circular drive and balconies off the top floors completing the showcase property.

Sol Santenelli had obviously done well for himself. Sarah came from money and a lifestyle completely different from Adam's.

Adam parked in the front drive, climbed out and opened her door for her, reaching down to grab her overnight bag. She tried to take it from him, but he snatched it.

"It's late, Sarah, and I know you're tired. Just go on inside."

A butler met them at the door. Seconds later, Sol Santenelli, a thin wiry man with graying hair and pale freckled skin, burst into the foyer, his cane thumping on the gleaming marble floor as he hastily strode toward Sarah.

"What are you doing here this late, sweetheart?" The older man gestured toward Adam. "And who's your friend?"

Sarah quickly signed an explanation. Judging from the horrified expression on her godfather's face and the way he swept her into a bear hug, she'd apparently told him about the attack.

"I told you not to talk to anyone," Santenelli said when he finally pulled away. "You've not only put yourself in danger, but now the CIRP will bear the brunt of this horrid publicity." He turned to Adam, the fine aging lines around his mouth tightening into a frown. "You can run along now, Detective. I'll take care of my goddaughter."

Adam stared him down. "Sir, I'll be back tomorrow to discuss the missing woman with Sarah."

"She doesn't know anything," Santenelli said. "She was confused from that medication. Leave her alone."

Adam had assumed Santenelli would be protective of Sarah, but he almost seemed hostile. Was Santenelli more concerned about Sarah's safety or the bad publicity for the research center?

Chapter Six

Sarah had no idea why her godfather was being so rude to Adam, but she felt the tension between the two men, as if two pit bulls had bared their teeth, preparing to engage in battle. Then again, maybe she was imagining things. Inside, she felt like a tightly coiled spring about to break any second.

"Sol, you should be thanking Detective Black," she signed. "He saved my life."

Sol's gray eyes darkened with emotions. He clasped her hand in his and bowed his head for a fraction of a second as if to collect himself.

"I appreciate what you did, Detective, and I hope you find the maniac who broke in. After all, my top priority is my goddaughter's safety."

"I can understand your concern, Mr. Santenelli, and you should check on her tonight." Adam indicated the bruise on her forehead. "She took a nasty hit there."

"Did you see a doctor, Sarah?"

"The paramedics said I'm fine," Sarah signed.

Sol aimed a worried look her way, then spoke to Adam. "I've been worried since she woke up in the hospital. She's had such a difficult time, Detective,

I'd hoped the hearing implants would change her life for the better, not resurrect bad memories.''

"They weren't memories," Sarah signed, irritated the men were talking over her as if she weren't present. "I heard a woman cry out for help. She may be Detective Black's sister, and I have to help if I can."

Sol's shocked expression darted to Adam. "Is this true? Is the woman your sister?"

Adam gave a curt nod. "Denise worked at the research center. The last time she was seen was the day Sarah had her surgery. Did you know her, Mr. Santenelli? Her name is Denise Harley."

"I recognize the name, but I don't know her personally." Sol scratched a finger along his brow. "I'm sorry to hear you can't find her. I hope she turns up, Detective Black. But I was in the hospital room with Sarah all night, and I didn't hear anything, so she had to be dreaming or hallucinating."

Sarah started to sign jerkily, but Sol curved an arm around her. "I'm just trying to take care of you, Sarah. You know I love you."

Sarah wavered. How could she argue with that? Sol had practically raised her. Naturally, his first loyalty would be to her. "I'll walk Detective Black to the door," she signed, daring Sol to argue.

He clamped his thin lips together. "Fine. I'll meet you in the study."

Sarah waited until Sol left, then turned to Adam. The heat flared again, subtle but simmering beneath the surface.

"I'd like you to go with me tomorrow to question Denise's husband."

Sarah frowned and mouthed, "Why?"

"He and Denise parted bitterly. I thought you might recognize his voice as the kidnapper."

So he believed her, Sarah thought, surprised. Especially after what Sol had said. She nodded her agreement, a sense of relief filling her. He raised his hand as if to touch her, then seemed to rein in whatever had prompted him to begin the gesture, turned and walked out the door. Sarah pressed her hand to her cheek, aching for his touch.

It was past midnight, but Adam sat on the deserted shore waiting on Clay to show, listening to the water lap against the sand and watching wave after wave crash onto the rocks. Sarah's face flashed into his mind. He wondered if Sarah missed the sound of the ocean. And other sounds he'd always taken for granted, like the sound of seagulls' cries and the wind playing its melody off the water. What must her life have been like?

Cold and silent? Living in a world all her own, haunted by traumatic memories of her parents' deaths? Knowing her father had actually killed her own mother?

Thankfully, she'd had her godfather. A rich and powerful man, influential in the scientific research world. A man who seemed to genuinely care for her. A man who'd taken her in when her father had been accused of treason, when he'd been labeled a murderer.

A man Adam had instantly disliked.

Maybe he disliked Santenelli because he had money, Adam reasoned. After all, he and Denise had been left with very little, except each other. He'd worried Denise wouldn't be able to pursue her dream of becoming a doctor, and he'd struggled to help her. In the end, they'd both scraped and borrowed to pay her way through school.

His gaze scanned the small corner of the island, then darted to the opposite side where the bulk of the research center's buildings were nestled, his emotions as tumultuous as the sea raging before a storm.

Where was his sister?

Was she alive? Being held on the island? Did her estranged husband have something to do with her disappearance? Or had there been a stalker? Had she probed into some confidential area at work that made others want to silence her?

Seashells crunched behind him, and his partner dropped down beside him. Stretching his long legs out, Clay's boots pushed the sand into a pile at his toes.

"Did you find anything at Denise's?" Adam asked.

"Some fingerprints, but we haven't identified them yet. How about at Sarah's?"

"None but hers and her godfather's."

Adam silently cursed. His least favorite part of police work—the waiting. "I'd like to look at her work files." Hell, he'd wanted to stay and search them when he'd first found her place ransacked, but his captain refused to let him be a part of the case and ordered him to leave.

Like anyone could stop him from being in on the case.

Clay harrumphed. "Wouldn't we all?"

Adam's pulse hammered. "You mean they're missing?"

"Didn't find any at her apartment."

He should have confiscated them the last time he

was there, Adam realized. But at the time he hadn't known if Denise's disappearance was work related. He doubted she kept confidential files at home anyway.

He had to get into her office.

The wind whistled behind his back, the salt air and scent of fish surrounding him. Tomorrow he'd find a way to get into the research center, right after he talked to Denise's husband.

Would Sarah's godfather help him gain access to her office, or would he stand in his way?

SARAH FACED SOL, her insides quaking at the drawn look on his face. "Sarah, are you all right?"

Tears clogged her throat, the evening almost too much. Her head had begun to pound on the way over, her muscles ached from struggling with her attacker, and her throat was so raw she could barely swallow. Still, she pasted on a brave face and signed, "Yes."

He wrapped his arms around her. "I don't know what I'd do if I lost you, sweetheart."

She hugged him back, nuzzling his neck as she'd done when she was a child, grateful for his unabiding love all through the years. His breath heaved out unevenly.

"I—I love you, Sarah. Please let this thing go."

She gently pulled away. "I'm tired, Sol. I'm going to take a hot bath and go to bed."

He lifted a fingerful of hair and tucked it behind her ear, reminding her of the tender father he'd always been. He'd attended her plays at the school for the deaf, taken her to the zoo, and although he was allergic to cats, he'd understood when she'd brought home Tigger, all injured and timid. "All right. Call if you need me. I'll have the maid send up some hot tea.''

''Thanks.'' She squeezed his hands, then watched as he hurried away to find Hilda. Exhausted, she walked toward the door, but the photo arrangement on the wall drew her eye and she stopped momentarily to study the pictures. In memory of her parents, Sol had placed photographs of them in the center. He'd emphasized that no matter what her father had done with the research, he'd loved Sarah.

She wished she could believe that.

In one picture, her mother and father stood beneath the branches of an oak, holding her. In the next her parents were at their wedding. Sol, serving as the best man, stood beside her father. Her parents seemed so in love. Why hadn't Sol ever married?

He'd always been so focused on work, so driven, she decided. Too driven for anyone but her. And he'd had nothing but wonderful things to say about her mother.

Not for the first time, Sarah's chest tightened, anguish filling her lungs. How could her father have betrayed them? How could he have killed her mother? Fisting her hands, she took several deep breaths, pushing the pain to the innermost corners of her mind.

Her gaze fell on the next picture, a group shot of several scientists on a fishing trip they'd taken the year before her father had died. Arnold Hughes, the CEO of the research center, had his arm thrown around her dad. Hughes had been her father's friend. He and Sol had remained friends and partners.

A chill suddenly rippled up her spine. During all the years she'd been around Arnold Hughes, she'd never felt comfortable with him, but she didn't understand why.

The psychiatrist she'd seen after the explosion had suggested she blamed him for exposing her father as a traitor. Maybe he was right. She hugged her arms around her middle and left the room, then climbed the winding staircase, promising herself tomorrow would be better.

Only tomorrow she had to accompany Adam Black to question his sister's husband.

She only hoped they found her.

Chapter Seven

It had been five long days since Adam had heard from Denise. Adam's temper flared at the sight of his sister's husband sitting calmly in the plush leather office chair in the house he and Denise had once shared. Sarah claimed a corner of the leather love seat, her hands folded neatly, her expression closed. Adam had introduced her as a friend, forgoing the details about her overhearing the kidnapping.

The soft-blue silk shell she wore outlined her luscious curves, while her long gauzy skirt hugged her slender legs. So far, she'd shown no sign she recognized Russell's voice.

"I told you Denise was obsessed with work. She stayed long hours, often forgot to call me or come home for dinner." Russell traced a long finger along the rim of a crystal water glass. "That's the reason we separated, Black. Sometimes I think her career was the only thing that mattered to her."

"Of course it mattered," Adam said in defense. "She worked her butt off to get through med school, and she felt damn lucky to have gotten a job at this high-tech research facility. She just wanted to impress her co-workers."

"No, Adam, she wanted to impress *you*."

Adam clamped his teeth together. "I never pushed her."

Russell sipped the water, staring over the rim of the glass with serious dark-green eyes. "Maybe, maybe not. Whatever the reason, she was an over-achiever."

"You know how she grew up."

Russell shrugged. "Yeah, but I wanted a *life,* too. And a wife who paid attention to me, not one who was married to her job."

"A little selfish, aren't you?"

Russell frowned. "Maybe. But work isn't every-thing. I learned that a long time ago." He stood and paced to the window, and stared out. "You see that tree out there?" He gestured toward a wooded area that had yet to be landscaped. "When we first bought this place, I imagined building a tree house for our son there. A swing set and sandbox and one of those jungle gyms." When he faced them again, Adam no-ticed the strain in his tight jaw. "But Denise didn't have time to make a family with me."

"And you were bitter about that?"

Anger blazed in Russell's eyes, but he shrugged, trying to act undisturbed. "Wouldn't you be?"

"Do you know where she is now?" Adam asked, ignoring the question.

"If you're suggesting I'd hurt Denise because I was angry, Black, you're way off base. I still love her." Russell dropped his head forward, looking weary. "My guess is she's holed up in a lab working on a cure for some rare disease we don't even know exists."

"You're not worried she hasn't called?"

Resignation softened Russell's eyes as he sat down. "I told you, I learned a long time ago not to expect anything from Denise."

Adam slapped a hand on the man's desk, sending a ballpoint pen rolling. "Don't you think it's suspicious that her apartment was broken into?"

For the first time since they'd arrived, fear crossed Russell's face. Fear for Denise or fear he'd been caught?

Russell winced at Denise's photo on his desk, and for a minute, Adam thought he detected true affection in Russell's eyes.

Or maybe he was just pretending.

"Was she there?" Russell asked, his voice gruff.

"No." Adam hesitated. "She hasn't been there for days, but it's too much of a coincidence that she's missing and her place was broken into. When was the last time you talked to her?"

"About two weeks ago. At the center."

"Do you know what kind of project she was working on?"

Russell pulled at his chin. "Like I told you, we didn't talk much. We exchanged pleasantries that day, that's all."

"Could you get me in her office to check around?"

"Security is damn near airtight. I'm in the marine department, which is in a separate area, so we'd have to get clearance. That'll take some time."

"Get on it. I want in there ASAP," Adam ordered. "What about co-workers? Did she get along with all of them, or ever mention having a problem with someone?"

"Not that I remember." A frown tightened his

face. "Although a while back, she mentioned that her new research assistant had a crush on her."

"What was his name?"

"Dan...no, Donny." Russell drummed his fingers in thought. "Donny Gates. He was a little younger than her, about five years, I think. Kind of a skinny guy with glasses. He seemed pretty harmless."

Adam had met a lot of people in his work who *seemed* harmless. Sometimes they were actually the most dangerous.

SARAH'S HEART bled for Adam. His love for his sister was so strong, she couldn't help but envy the other woman. She desperately wanted to ask about his parents, to find out more about his and Denise's childhoods, and she cursed herself for not being able to communicate.

"Did his voice sound familiar?" Adam asked as soon as they got in the car.

Sarah used her Palm Pilot to reply. "I'm not sure. I don't think it was the man I heard, but the voices from the hospital were muffled." And she had been drugged. "Do you think he was telling the truth?"

"I don't know," Adam admitted quietly. "At first when he and Denise married, he adored her, or at least he seemed to."

Sarah's heart squeezed. He looked so bereft she reached out and lay a hand over his, then stroked his fingers. Adam stared at their hands on the seat, a muscle ticking in his jaw.

"I have to find her," he finally said in a tortured voice. His dark gaze lifted to meet hers. "And she's not the coldhearted woman Russell painted her to be.

She's dedicated and brilliant, and she's worked hard to make it.''

Sarah smiled, then wrote, "I know. She sounds wonderful."

"She was…is. You'd have to understand how hard it was for her," Adam said, emotion thickening his voice. "When our parents died in that car crash, she was only thirteen. Overnight, she changed from a smart girl to a withdrawn, shy kid." Sarah laced her fingers with his, waiting, letting him pour out his heart.

"I promised Mom and Dad I'd take care of her, I swore it on their graves. And her dream was to be a doctor. That's all she ever talked about."

Sarah nodded. "I can understand that. When I lost my family, I was young, but once I decided to teach, my life had focus."

His dark eyes swept over her with admiration, making Sarah's heart swell. She'd grown accustomed to curious looks and pitying glances, not sincere respect for her accomplishments.

Or a man looking at her with heat in his eyes the way Adam did.

As if she recognized the subtle tension had begun simmering between them again, he turned away, started the engine and pulled down the long drive. "I have to check out Russell's story about the research assistant. Mind coming along to see if his voice sounds familiar?"

Sarah shook her head. "Not if you think it might help find your sister."

Adam's fists clenched around the steering wheel. "I don't know if it will or not, but I have to do something. Every day she's missing lessens the chances of us finding her alive."

Chapter Eight

As Adam headed toward the research center on Cat-call Island, troubled thoughts lurched back and forth in his head like the tide rolling in and out off the coast.

He did not want to like Sarah. And he especially didn't want to admire her. At least when he'd believed she was a kook, he could ignore her bewitching eyes. He'd be crazy to consider a relationship with her other than the professional one they already shared.

She was fragile, both physically and emotionally. So scarred, she still couldn't speak.

What would a frail woman like her think if he ever unleashed the powerful emotions raging inside him? She deserved fine wines and candlelight dinners, not pizza and beer with a run-down cop. God only knew the types of lowlifes he dealt with. How could he share stories about his day with someone as sheltered as her?

No.

Getting physical with Sarah would no doubt mean attachments—she just wasn't a one-night stand kind of woman.

He'd joined the police department so he could protect vulnerable people like her, not get involved with them.

Yet you couldn't even protect your own sister.

Grief and failure suffused him, but he fought it, reminding himself he wasn't finished yet. He would find Denise. And he'd use Sarah Cutter to help him if he had to.

SARAH WATCHED Adam struggle with his temper as he tried to locate Denise's research assistant. He leaned over the top of the receptionist's computer, enunciating each word slowly. "His name is Donny Gates."

"Like I told you a few days ago, he's not here," the thin receptionist chirped.

"When will he be back?"

"I'm not sure. Since Dr. Harley left town, he hasn't been in much. Just to pick up some samples for his project. I'm sure when she returns, he'll be back, too. He seemed pretty dedicated to her."

"Dedicated or obsessed?"

The woman seemed surprised. "I'm not sure what you mean."

"Could he have wanted more than a working relationship with her? Was he obsessed with my sister?"

"I—I really don't know." She tucked an errant strand of hair into place. "I don't stick my nose into other people's business, Detective."

"Look, lady, don't tell me you didn't notice—"

"If you're going to shout at me, Detective Black, I'm calling security."

Sarah lay a hand on Adam's arm to calm him. He

inhaled sharply, but lowered his voice when he spoke again. "When will my sister be back?"

The receptionist tapped the calendar. "My notations indicate she'll be gone two more weeks."

Adam cursed, and Sarah shifted nervously behind him. She understood his frustration but felt helpless as how to make things better.

"Then give me Gates's home address and phone number," Adam demanded.

"I can't do that," the woman said, looking panicky. "It's against Seaside Securities's policy."

"Then I'll find it myself." Adam slammed a hand on the counter. "I'll be back with a search warrant, and next time I won't let your security company get in my way."

SARAH CUTTER probably thought he was a bastard, Adam thought, as he drove like a maniac toward the central office of the center to see her godfather. She'd just have to go on thinking it though, because he didn't give a damn who he pissed off or if the researchers were cloning the President. This stupid research company would not keep him from finding Denise.

"I hope your godfather will cooperate," Adam told her as he parked in front of the two-story building. "Then I'd like to see the room where you had your surgery."

Sarah nodded, watching him quietly, her big blue eyes glistening with emotions he dared not pursue. She seemed so intuitive, so compassionate, that he forgot sometimes that she couldn't even talk. That they could barely communicate.

Except they'd communicated pretty well during that kiss.

He had to forget that kiss.

Glancing sideways, he noticed her rubbing small circles around her temple as if she had a headache. Unwanted guilt slammed into him. The woman had a slight concussion, yet he'd dragged her all over the island without bothering to stop for lunch. He kept forgetting her fragile state.

"Do you want to get lunch before we do this?"

She shook her head, then wrote, "Maybe later."

"Your head okay?" All right, so maybe he did care if she thought he was a bastard. He wasn't completely heartless.

Probably because he'd been a big brother for so long. He'd always taken care of his little sister, so he felt indebted to take care of Sarah. Except his thoughts toward her weren't brotherly.

A small smile curved her lips. "I've got a buzz in my ears that's making it hard to hear, but I've had worse."

He nodded and hurried to her side to open the door, but she'd climbed out by the time he reached her.

They walked in silence up the pebbled drive, the scent of the salt air wafting around them with the early-afternoon breeze. Sun beamed on the modern stucco structure, the Wilmington River rippling behind them. A beautiful place for a business. But had something menacing happened here?

Seconds later, thanks to Sarah's relationship to Sol Santenelli, they were seated in his office. The view of the river through the floor-length glass windows astounded Adam. Medical journals filled cherry bookshelves on the opposite wall, a seating area with thick leather furniture occupied one corner, a stocked wet bar the other. Adam couldn't imagine working in such ritzy surroundings.

Santenelli offered them drinks. Adam took coffee, Sarah a soda. Santenelli settled into an expensive dark swivel chair. "How are you today, Sarah?"

She smiled and signed something that Adam assumed meant she was fine. She certainly wasn't a whiner, he thought, that seed of admiration growing.

"I want clearance to see the Coastal Island Research Park," Adam said without preamble. "And I'd like to see the hospital room where Sarah had her surgery."

Santenelli twisted his mouth sideways, looking grim. "Why should I give you access to restricted areas when you have no proof your sister is really missing?"

Sarah signed frantically.

"Whoa, Sarah, I can't read you that fast," Santenelli said.

She repeated the movements, and Adam watched her godfather's face contort. "Yes, I want you to have peace of mind, Sarah, but I think you're out on a limb here, and I don't want to jeopardize the research center's reputation or their research for some unfounded claim." He turned to Adam. "You don't know for sure that something has happened to your sister, do you?"

Although he had no evidence, Adam knew it in his gut. "Yes, she's missing. And I've already put in for a court order to search the facility."

Santenelli steepled his fingers on the desk. "All right. I'll see what I can do about getting you into the lab areas. That may take a day or two. But I can show you the hospital where Sarah stayed right now.''

''All right.'' Adam stood abruptly. ''Let's go.''

SARAH SHIVERED as she entered the research hospital and followed her godfather and Adam through the corridor, the hospital smells engulfing her, resurrecting memories of the numerous surgeries she'd had during her childhood, of the hope she'd felt before she'd received the implants.

Remembering the last time she'd been here and the panicked cries of the woman being abducted.

Noises bombarded her—voices paging various doctors over the intercom, the beep of a machine as they passed a room, the sounds of gurneys rolling down the hall, two people arguing.

She rubbed her temple, then hesitated in the hallway near the elevator, a dizzy spell assaulting her, the faint murmur of a man's voice ringing in her ears. Then static.

''Sarah, are you all right?'' Adam Black's warm hand steadied her, his husky voice a reprieve from the grating sounds around her.

She nodded, determined not to show any signs of weakness. Was the man's voice the one she'd heard kidnapping Denise? She strained for the sound, but a garbled noise reverberated in her ear.

''Should we have you checked, sweetheart?'' Sol asked.

She signed, ''No,'' then waved for them to continue.

Seconds later, they entered the second floor where she'd had her surgery. The whitewashed walls and gleaming stainless steel hospital bed looked exactly as she remembered.

"This hospital is used strictly for patients undergoing experimental procedures and treatments?" Adam asked.

Sol nodded. "Yes, it was built especially for the center and houses a variety of specialties, although most of the doctors have separate labs in another building for their research work. Sarah's hearing implants were performed in the surgical wing. She stayed in another room afterward for observation."

The hospital resembled any other, housed with the same basic layout and furniture. A hospital bed, dinner tray, chair for visitors, overhead TV, blinds, a private bath.

His big body moved silently as he crossed to stare at the vent overhead. "What floor is neurology?"

Sol's eyebrows narrowed. "I believe it's on the next floor. Why?"

"That's where my sister worked." He jerked his head up, gesturing toward the ceiling. "So, it's conceivable that Sarah did hear something that night. The sound could have carried through the vent."

ADAM WAS CERTAIN now that Sarah had heard his sister being abducted. Only he had no idea who had taken Denise or why or where they had taken her.

They had combed the hospital corridors, yet he hadn't found anyone who corroborated her story, and Sarah hadn't matched any of the voices of the people they'd met with the man she'd heard. After a strained and silent dinner at a local Italian café, he'd gotten Donny Gates's home address from Clay, and they'd driven to the research assistant's rental home on Skidaway Island, but Gates hadn't been home. Sarah looked exhausted.

She slipped into her apartment, her face paling at the sight of the dusty room—he'd forgotten how jarring it was for a victim to face the crime scene, how violated she must feel now to see her personal domain touched by violence.

"A consultant is adding extra security to your place," Adam told her. "They'll be here tomorrow."

She thumbed through the stack of mail on the sofa table and nodded absently, her small shoulders slumped with fatigue. He placed his hands on her arms, sucking in a sharp breath at the heat that shot through him. She tensed, then looked up at him. Her beautiful blue eyes shimmered with an awareness that mirrored his own attraction, yet the bruise on her forehead and neck jolted him back to reality.

"Go rest for a while. I'll clean up this mess."

She started to shake her head in refusal, that streak of independence flaring, but he caught her chin with his hand. "Yes, Sarah. You have a slight concussion and I've dragged you nonstop over the island today. You need to rest."

Helpless to restrain himself, he traced a line down her delicate jawbone. "I'm staying here tonight, so you'll be safe."

For a brief second, alarm flitted in her eyes.

"I'll sleep on the couch. That is, unless you'd rather go back to your godfather's tonight."

She shook her head no as he'd expected. Before they'd left Santenelli, her godfather had urged her to return to his house, but she'd firmly expressed her need to go home. Her independence reminded him of Denise and the way he used to butt heads with her.

Santenelli's nostrils had flared with anger at Sarah's refusal to stay, and Adam realized what it must have cost her to fight for herself against his powerful presence.

Of course, he admitted begrudgingly, he also understood her godfather's need to protect her. A man had to stay in control, take care of the people he loved, especially the women. His father had taught him that. Hell, his mother had liked being taken care of. She'd lost her sight a year before she'd died and had become even more dependent than ever. But his father hadn't minded taking care of her.

With a small sigh, Sarah covered his hand with her own, her soft skin brushing his, charging his nerve endings with electricity. For a brief second, her gaze dropped to his mouth and he saw need and desire written plainly on her face. Heat spread through him, blazing in its intensity.

But he could not, would not follow through, not when she looked so physically weak and vulnerable.

Her fingers laced his, and she squeezed his hand so tenderly that he heard the unspoken message. They didn't need words to communicate. She shared his need for comfort, for a soft touch, yet she also understood his reservations. And in that moment he realized she wasn't the needy, vulnerable, fragile woman he'd thought, or maybe the one he'd wanted her to be.

Sarah was strong and gutsy. So strong she'd overcome a traumatic past and a hearing impairment to live a normal, productive life. Even more admirable, she'd stepped forward to help a virtual stranger while putting her own life in danger.

The realization made him want her more.

But he couldn't act on that want.

Getting involved would make him lose focus, and that might put her in even more danger. Just like it had with Pamela. He'd let his defenses slip for a minute and she had ended up dead.

"Go rest, Sarah," he said in a gruff voice.

She nodded and left him with a small smile on her lips and a look of want so powerful he was tempted to follow her.

But he didn't.

He silently vowed to protect her, even if it meant walking away from her.

SARAH TRIED TO REST and forget about the electrifying tension between her and Adam, but when she stretched out on her bed, memories of the horrifying attack assaulted her. Would she ever feel safe in here again?

Adam Black was in the other room, she reminded herself. For now, at least she could relax. And she would learn to be on her own again once this nightmare ended.

But how was she supposed to sleep with Adam lying in the other room on her sofa?

Unbidden images sprang to her mind, filling her with another kind of tension. Images of Adam next to her, folding her in his arms, slowly unbuttoning her blouse, slipping her skirt down her legs, then sliding her panties off and twining his body with hers.

She had never slept with a man before.

Had never wanted or lusted after a man the way she lusted after Adam. He made her feel strong and safe and utterly feminine. Yet she sensed he thought her handicap made her too vulnerable. As had her former boyfriend.

Why couldn't Adam see beneath the impairment to the strong woman inside?

Good heavens, what was she thinking anyway?

She didn't need to get involved with him. Adam Black was a detective, his life so different from hers that there was no chance they'd ever have a real relationship. The only reason he'd assigned himself as her protector was duty and his determination to find Denise.

Her head throbbed and a slight ringing echoed in her ears. She closed her eyes, massaging her temple with her fingertips. Was there something wrong with the implants or was she simply exhausted from all the sounds and the tension of looking for Denise?

She turned off her Tiffany bedside lamp and closed her eyes, envisioning cool breezes and the sounds of the ocean playing off the rocks at night. She'd heard it today when they'd driven along the coast. Slowly, the pain began to recede and she felt herself drifting into a light sleep.

But soon, a jangling noise intruded on her peace.

She jerked her eyes open, surveying the room, trying to discern the source of the sound. The ringing sounded again—the doorbell. No, this was different.

Adam walked inside and stood beside her bed, then gestured toward the phone and she noticed the light flashing. "Do you want me to answer it?"

She nodded and he punched the speakerphone button.

A nasally voice filtered over the line. "Ms. Cutter, this is Robey Burgess. I guess you saw my article by now." He paused, but Sarah was helpless to reply, so he continued. "I know you and that cop are snooping around the research center, and I know he's there with you now. Just thought you'd like to know that that woman you heard cry out for help isn't the first scientist who turned up missing.

"Last year a microbiologist named Jerome Simms was on the verge of some cutting edge research regarding the disposal of hazardous wastes. Guess what happened to him?"

"What?" Adam asked, angry Burgess had been watching them.

"He turned up dead."

Chapter Nine

"How did he die?" Adam asked.

"I thought that would get your interest. Is Ms. Cutter there?"

"Yes, but she can't come to the phone."

"She's listening though, right?"

"It doesn't matter. Now, how did Simms die?"

"Supposedly a boating accident," Burgess said. "But Simms was an expert swimmer and diver. Sounds suspicious, doesn't it?"

Adam gritted his teeth, hating to agree with anything the slimy tabloid reporter said. "It's interesting."

"Interesting, hell, it's too coincidental and you know it. I'd like to strike a deal—"

"I don't deal with reporters," Adam said.

"I was talking about a deal with Ms. Cutter."

"You expect her to trust a sleazeball who printed garbage about her and put her in danger?"

"She should have told me the truth. After what happened with her old man, I thought she'd want to know that Simms was about to sell his research to a foreign government." Burgess whistled. "Sounds familiar, doesn't it, Ms. Cutter? You wanna talk now?"

Sarah flinched.

Adam exhaled, battling his temper. "She's not interested, Mr. Burgess, now leave Sarah alone."

"I could help you crack this open—"

"I don't need help. I do my own investigating." Adam punched off the phone, cutting off the man's reply.

A haunted look darkened Sarah's eyes. He pulled her hands into his, hating the reporter for hurting her. Her fingers were so cold he rubbed them with his own, trying to warm them.

As much as he hated to admit it, Simms's death sounded suspicious. He had to wonder if somehow it paralleled his sister's disappearance.

ONCE AGAIN Sarah struggled to sleep, this time her rest was disturbed by images of death. The microbiologist. Her mother. Her father.

Adam's sister.

Her.

The attacker had returned. This time, he'd bound and gagged her and tied her to a chair. The smell of gasoline assaulted her, and she watched in horror as he poured gas from a metal can into a circle around her. Through the slits in the ski mask, his piercing eyes darted up to her and a smile curled his lips. He was laughing, taking pleasure in his game.... Why?

Who was he? Why did he want to kill her?

And why couldn't she stop him? Why couldn't she cry out for help?

Adam's sister, a petite version of the man, dark hair, olive skin, drifted toward her. No! Denise was walking into the flames as if she couldn't see them. Oh, God. Her father was standing behind Denise.

Sarah had to save her. To yell her name.

She opened her mouth to scream, but fear trapped the sound in her throat. Thick, cold terror paralyzed her, just like the day her mother had died.

Flames burst around her, eating the wooden floor, sucking the oxygen from the air, scalding her skin....

The voices returned. A man's. Low, threatening. Denise's cry. Soft, anguished.

She bolted upward, tears streaming down her face. What was happening to her? Was she losing her mind?

Adam suddenly pulled her into his arms, crooning soft words.

"Shh, it's all right, Sarah. You're safe now."

She curled against him, soaking up his warmth, praying he was right, that his sister hadn't died. That her father hadn't been there. No, he was dead.

And she was selfishly grateful she was alive.

And in Adam's arms, she felt more alive than she ever had before.

All her life she'd been treated differently because of her hearing impairment. She didn't want to be considered weak, defective. She wanted to feel desirable, like a whole woman. Like Adam's woman.

She lifted her hand and sought comfort by pressing her lips to Adam's. He met her mouth with a low growl, then dragged her into his arms and licked at her lips with his tongue. His kiss was hungry, almost savage as he thrust his tongue inside her mouth, tasting every corner, greedily taking all she had to offer. Sarah arched her neck and clung to him, matching his hunger with her own fierce need. His big hands splayed across her back, touching her everywhere, cupping her face to angle her mouth for a deeper kiss, stroking her hair, the sensitive skin of her neck, rubbing her arms, her waist, then roaming to her breasts.

Sarah's body tingled with desire, her nipples tightening beneath the satiny barrier of her gown. She whimpered softly, clenching her hands around his taut muscles as he dipped his head and began to lave her neck with his tongue. He sipped and kissed the sensitive skin behind her ear, then traced a fiery path down her neck, lower, until he'd jerked open the top button of her nightshirt and his mouth sucked the curve of her breasts.

Liquid heat pooled in her belly. Sarah dug her nails into his arms, hanging on for the most intense ride she could ever imagine.

But suddenly he stopped. Her breath rushed out, ragged and torn, her heart pounded in rapid beats as he pulled away and stared at the opening of her shirt. Her breasts weren't large, but neither were they small, and they swelled beneath his heated gaze, aching for his touch.

He dragged his gaze up to her mouth, then her eyes, a look of pure raw hunger brimming in the depths, yet she also saw regret and some other emotion banked in his gaze. What was he thinking?

She mouthed the word, ''What?''

He tugged her shirt together and buttoned the top button, his fingers shaking. The pain of his withdrawal left a chill inside her that resurrected all the times other men had found her lacking.

''I'm sorry, Sarah. That was a mistake.'' He stood, his back rigid as he turned to collect himself. With a guttural sound from deep in his throat, he stalked from the room, leaving her cold and alone.

Sarah knew she should let him go, but she'd fought

for independence all her life and had never backed down from a fight. She wouldn't now.

Adam stared out the window, the black, starless sky mirroring his dark mood. Sarah had a nightmare, had needed comfort, but a comforting embrace had turned into something else.

He heard her footsteps padding on the carpet and closed his eyes, steeling himself against her reaction. She would have regrets in the morning, maybe blame him for taking advantage of the situation.

She tugged at his arm, and he slowly turned to face her, his apology forming in his mind. She looked angry all right, her eyes blazing, her lips parted, her cheeks rosy-red.

Or were her cheeks grazed from his crude near-lovemaking?

She thrust her Palm Pilot toward him with a trembling hand. He studied her for a moment, his gut clenching at the vulnerable look in her eyes. Finally he dropped his gaze and read, ''Why did you stop?''

His gaze swung to her, and he watched her fold her arms across her chest. She couldn't know that the movement only accentuated her breasts and made his hunger grow.

''I—I let things get out of control. I'm sorry.'' He rammed a hand through his hair, sending the overly long strands in disarray. ''I told you I wouldn't touch you again and I broke my promise.''

She exhaled a shaky breath, then wrote. ''I never asked you for that promise. I never asked you to stop.''

She couldn't know what she was saying. ''Look, Sarah, you're too damn innocent for me.''

''Innocent?'' she mouthed.

''Yes.'' He stared at her, seeing the truth in the

emotions flitting in her eyes. "You are, aren't you? You've never been with a man?"

"It doesn't matter," Sarah scribbled. "I could feel the heat between us. You can't deny that."

He cursed. She *was* a virgin. If she'd waited that long to be with a man, it should be perfect. It should be with the man she wanted to marry. He didn't fit that bill at all. "I can't deny we have chemistry. I'm a man and you're a beautiful woman, but sex and love have nothing to do with each other. And what you and I have is lust, honey, pure and simple lust."

Her dark eyebrow rose.

"You—you're vulnerable, Sarah, too damn soft for a man like me. For God's sake, you just had surgery, someone tried to kill you and you've been traumatized…." He threw up his hands in frustration. "And I have to find my sister. I don't have time for a personal relationship right now. Or ever. So, go back to bed and leave me alone."

She raised a hand to write a reply, but he cut her off, knowing he had to say something to convince her. He just wasn't the man for her. She needed a nicer, stable guy who'd come home to her every night with flowers and candy, not a jaded detective who had nothing to offer her.

"Think about it, Sarah, you're too fragile for me. My life is my job and that's the way I like it."

Hurt flickered on her face, slamming guilt into his already confused soul, then she turned and walked into her bedroom, leaving him alone, just as he'd requested.

SARAH HAD WANTED to hear for years, but right now, she wished she could block out the harsh words Adam had just muttered. Because those words confirmed every worst fear she had, every insecurity, every dash of hope that a normal, strong man like Adam would want her. Hadn't she learned anything from her college boyfriend?

He'd refused to make love to her because he was afraid she would get pregnant, that they might have an imperfect child or that she wouldn't be a good mother because she couldn't hear.

Furious with herself for confronting Adam, she tried to pull herself together.

She would not cry over Adam Black.

She'd had worse things happen in her life than enduring a man's rejection, and she would survive. She would also make sure they kept their relationship work oriented from now on. Just as he wanted.

Yes, she'd do her best to help him find his sister, then he would be out of her life for good.

LONG AFTER Sarah went to bed, Adam sat in front of his laptop, trying to forget the hurt look in Sarah's eyes, and searched for information on the microbiologist, Jerome Simms. Apparently the man's research focused on the role of microbes in the cleanup of hazardous wastes. After his death, reporters speculated that he'd uncovered some mishandling of wastes by the research center, implying that the soil and waters nearby could be contaminated. It had also been speculated that he'd developed a new synthetic compound. If the center wanted to cover it up, they could have killed him.

However, nothing was found to substantiate the claims, the research center cooperated with the investigation and the man's death had been deemed accidental.

The report was short and to the point, but offered nothing concrete, nothing that satisfied Adam. Government cover-ups had happened before. Could they have happened here in the coastal area?

Still, even if the microbiologist had been killed because of some fluke discovery, his sister hadn't been working with microbes or the environment. The last he knew, she worked in neurology, researching a cure for Alzheimer's.

Finally, deciding he'd done all he could until he searched Denise's office, he stretched out on Sarah's blue-flowered couch, frowning at her ceramic cat collection, the lace doilies on the fragile antique sofa table, the romance novels and children's books on the shelves. He'd never met anyone like Sarah Cutter.

She was such an odd mixture of sweetness and toughness...and sexuality. Her house, her job, her good nature all screamed of family and hearth and home. Of commitment.

While his only commitment was to his job.

But her soft, sultry dark hair and luscious curves made his mouth water. And those eyes—those vibrant, beautiful eyes had secrets in their depths, secrets of a hunger she'd long denied, of a passionate woman ready to give herself to a man. But it should be the right man. Not him. Unfortunately when that heated look touched him, his honorable intentions disintegrated.

He could hear her voice in his thoughts, a voice he imagined sounding like the soft, husky strains of a blues singer, a voice that would sing to his soul and whisper erotic promises in the night.

A voice, that though silent, would splinter his emotions as well as his heart if he let it. Was she undressing now, running her fingers over the pale soft skin that he wanted to touch? Combing her hands through those long dark tresses that he imagined skimming across his bare belly when they made love?

Frustrated, he cursed and stared at the ceiling, knowing he probably couldn't sleep tonight for thinking about the two women in his life—his sister whom he dearly loved but couldn't find, and Sarah, the woman he wanted but couldn't have.

CLAYTON CALLED the next morning to say he had obtained the court order, giving Adam access to CIRP's research facilities. They would have to be accompanied by someone from Seaside Securities, but at least he could get into Denise's office.

And the private security company had finally sent a consultant over to install a system in Sarah's apartment.

"I want the best system you can put in." Adam ignored Sarah's glare.

"We'll take care of it today," the man agreed.

Sarah handed the consultant a note. "Bill me for the system."

Adam frowned, sensing the tension between them had as much to do with the night before as the fact that he'd taken control over her safety. They drove in silence, his thoughts replaying the morning. Sarah had barely acknowledged him at breakfast, making him feel about two feet tall for the way he'd acted the night before, but one day she'd realize he was right. She'd be glad he hadn't taken her virginity and left her in the dust with broken promises and bitterness between them.

Bill Wood, a burly man with a dark mole on his left cheek and shiny gold rings on four fingers waved them through security at CIRP and led them to Denise's office and the connected lab. Dr. Bradford gave them a guided tour of the facility, pointing out the various labs, explaining that some of the security measures had been installed to keep the public safe. CIRP also had projects located in another building and one on Nighthawk Island which required special decontamination measures, so those were off-limits. Adam spotted nothing out of the ordinary, other than a few gray doors which were sealed and required special approval to enter. Of course, he sensed they were seeing only what Bradford and Seaside Securities had approved for them to see. Finally, Wood escorted them to Denise's office and the adjoining lab.

"Your sister was working on a project to aid in the cure of Alzheimer's," Bradford explained, elaborating slightly.

"Is that the only project she was involved with?" Adam asked.

"It was her top priority."

Sarah studied the facility, but she hadn't reacted to Bradford's voice, so Adam assumed he probably wasn't the man who'd abducted Denise. Clay probed through a few of the metal drawers, frowning when they revealed standard lab equipment.

"Can we see Denise's research assistant's desk?" Adam asked.

Bradford looked perplexed, but Wood unlocked the desk. Adam scoured through it. Notes about Alzheimer's, several kinds of experimental drugs, a log of facilities willing to test the drugs in clinical trials—everything he'd expect to find. Disappointed, he asked to see Gates's locker.

Adam grimaced as the metal door swung. On the inside of the door, the research assistant had taped dozens of snapshots of Denise. And judging from some of the compromising shots, she hadn't known Gates had taken them.

Chapter Ten

"I had no idea." Dr. Bradford's expression of shock mirrored the horror Sarah felt at seeing the shrine of photos. A few were candid shots of Denise at work bent over a microscope. Another photo showed her climbing from her car, but a more disturbing one followed. Denise lay in bed wearing a shimmering green nightgown. Even more upsetting, the photo had obviously been taken by someone looking in through her window.

Did Denise have any idea her assistant had been infatuated with her? That he had violated her privacy by spying on her?

Adam's normally bronze complexion paled beneath the fluorescent lights. Bradford reached out to pull one of the pictures from the door, but Adam stopped him.

"We need to photograph it for evidence," he explained, his voice gruff with emotions. "Where is Gates?"

Bradford looked rattled. "I assumed Denise gave him a couple of weeks off since she wasn't going to be around."

Sarah hugged her arms around her waist, aching to

reach out and comfort Adam. He squared his shoulders, his mask of professional detachment in place, but she knew he must be hurting inside. She had never met Denise, yet she could hardly bear the thought of how the woman might be suffering.

What if Donny Gates had revealed his feelings to Denise, and she had rejected him? Could he have gone over the edge and kidnapped her and... No, she couldn't think like that. They had to find the woman; her cries lingered in Sarah's mind. She had felt Denise's fear. She had to see her alive.

Clay phoned the crime lab. "We may be able to match his fingerprints with some found in Denise's apartment."

"Right. And I want a full background check done on Gates, all his priors," Adam said. "Get his mental history back to when he was born."

"I'll take care of it," Clay said.

"I'm taking Sarah to her godfather's house, then I'm going to Gates's apartment."

"I'll call for a search warrant and meet you there," Clay said.

"I'll go with you," Sarah wrote.

Adam shook his head. "No, if Gates is there, it might get dangerous. I want you someplace safe."

"But what if I can identify his voice?"

"Once we have him in custody, I'll send for a car. You can come to the station and ID him."

"Then take me home."

"No, I don't want you to be alone," Adam said in a low voice. "You'll be safer at your godfather's."

Sarah heard the air of authority in his voice and hated relinquishing control of her life. But she didn't have a death wish, either, so she relented, vowing to protect herself the only way she knew how, by retreating into her silence.

ADAM HAD NO IDEA that time could move so slowly, but the drive to Gates's small rental house seemed like an eternity. Twisted images from past cases filled his mind. He prayed Denise had not met the same fate as some of the stalker victims he'd seen on file.

Thankfully, Sarah was safe, and Clay had pushed to get a search warrant so by the time he dropped Sarah at Santenelli's and arrived on Skidaway at Gates's rental house, they could search the place.

He would have broken in if he'd had to.

He just prayed they found evidence that Gates hadn't killed her.

The house sat on a patch of land that smelled of the marsh, its lawn dry and overgrown with weeds, the shabby exterior exhibiting evidence of the damage salt air and tropical storms could inflict on painted wood.

He knocked on the weathered door three times, then called out, identifying himself and Clayton as the police. Not surprised when no one answered, he jimmied the worn lock and slammed his weight against the thin wood, knocking it open the second time.

Darkness shadowed the interior, hazy lines of sunshine slanting across the room through the miniblinds.

"Gates, it's the police," Clayton called out again. "If you're here, show yourself now."

Adam waited, his hand clenching his weapon. Several seconds passed, tension filling the air, yet no one appeared. Finally, Clayton flicked on the overhead light.

Adam scanned the room. Although the carpet and furniture appeared old, the air of neatness about the room suggested Gates either had a daily maid or an obsessive-compulsive disorder. Magazines were arranged alphabetically on racks, as were CDs. Pillows sat at precisely matching angles. Pictures of shellfish and sea organisms lined one wall near a six-foot aquarium of exotic fish.

Not too odd for a research assistant, he supposed. But something seemed off.

Clay moved to the kitchen while Adam slowly combed the bedroom and bath. The bed was meticulously made, three towels hung at exactly the same levels.

So far, no sign of Gates or Adam's sister.

But the scent of death hung in the stale, cold air.

His lungs tightened as he moved to the spare bedroom. A neat desk, topped with a meticulously labeled file organizer occupied one corner. A tall swivel chair faced the wall, the back of the chair faced toward Adam so he couldn't see if it was occupied. His gut instinct told him something was terribly wrong here. The foul odor grew stronger as he approached the chair. His stomach rolled when he spotted a wall of pictures in the corner by the man's desk—all pictures of Denise.

He circled the chair and his heart pounded.

Gates was slumped over in the chair, his head dropped forward, his chin resting on his drool-stained shirt, a hypodermic on the desk, a piece of paper in his hand. Adam knew without looking that it was probably a suicide note.

WHAT WOULD ADAM find at Donny Gates's apartment, Sarah wondered? More pictures? Something to tell him where Denise was being held?

Something to confirm she was still alive?

Her own nerves on alert, Sarah found the maid and begged some hot tea, then tried to relax in the den, but the comments that reporter had made about the microbiologist's death and her father's disturbed her. He'd hinted that there might be a connection or at least a similarity between their stories. Both had intended to sell their findings to a foreign government. Both had ended up dead with their reputations damaged.

She wanted to talk to Sol. He would tell her the truth. A noise, full of static, filled her ears and she pressed her hands over them, trying to discern the sound. A man's voice? A woman's? The sounds broke and faded.

What in the world was happening to her? Could she still be hearing Denise and the man?

"Do you want to rest upstairs for a while, Ms. Cutter?" Hilda asked.

Sarah shook herself back to the present and signed, "No, I'll wait in the study. I want to talk to my godfather when he gets home."

"Fine, just let me know if you need anything."

Sarah thanked her and took the steaming cup of Earl Grey to her godfather's study, her gaze taking in the wall of bookshelves filled with research material and reference books. Sol also had a small collection of leather-bound classics along with golfing books. He'd sworn when he retired he'd become a pro golfer, but Sarah had laughed. Her godfather had never excelled at sports, only in academics. He'd been ruthless in negotiating contracts for the research center and was known for being able to entice financial support from the most reluctant entrepreneur. He even kept scrapbooks of all his deals and the various companies he had helped to get off the ground.

She removed several of the scrapbooks from the shelf and began to thumb through them. A few clippings identified smaller research companies she hadn't heard of, most of them medically related. Finally, she found the book containing articles about the hearing device her father had been working on. The first two praised his work for the government, but offered no details about the hearing device.

The photo of her godfather and Arnold Hughes drew her eye and she shivered again, wondering again why Hughes made her feel so uncomfortable.

Fresh pain cut through her, but she forced herself to read the damning articles about her parents' death, her eyes blurring with tears at the pictures of their burned house, the two gray caskets, the graveyard. She barely realized she was crying, but the tears dripped down her cheeks onto the plastic covering the photos. Reaching sideways for a tissue from the end table, the scrapbook slipped and fell from her lap. She retrieved the book, but a folded, yellowed newspaper clipping slid from beneath one of the pages, the article dated 1982, a year after her parents' deaths. Curious, she opened the faded paper, a gasp escaping her at the headline: ''Research scientist and suspected treasonist Charles Cutter, who was accused of murdering his wife and setting the explosion which caused his own daughter's hearing loss, is thought to be alive.''

Chapter Eleven

"Nothing in the kitchen." Clay entered the spare bedroom, stopping abruptly at the sight of Gates's body. "Oh, damn."

Adam leaned his head into his hands, frustration and panic clawing at him.

"Suicide?" Clay asked quietly.

"Looks that way."

Clay's gaze landed on the shrine of photographs. "Holy mother of—" Clay caught himself. "I wonder if Denise knew."

Or if she found out the hard way, Adam thought, hearing the unspoken question. Maybe she'd rejected Gates and he had snapped. Worse, what if he'd taken her whereabouts with him to his grave? "I can't believe the SOB was such a coward he killed himself," Adam said.

Clay made a disgusted sound. "Fits the profile of these sickos."

Knowing he dare not contaminate the evidence, Adam used a handkerchief to lift the note and read it.

"I loved you, Denise. I can't live knowing you don't want me. I'm sorry we couldn't finish the research together. But we will be together now. Because there is only love in heaven. Forever and always. Love, Donny.''

"I'll have the crime lab analyze it," Clay said, "make sure it was typed on his computer, see if there are any other prints.''

Emotions overpowered Adam as the meaning of the note sank in.

THE ARTICLE trembled in Sarah's hands as she read on.

New evidence has come to light in the mystery surrounding Charles Cutter, a scientist on the cutting edge of research for the U.S. government. Evidence corroborates the fact that he was negotiating to sell copies of a high-tech listening device to the Russians when his wife and a co-worker discovered his intentions. While Cutter was believed to have died in the explosion that killed his wife and injured his daughter, police now believe that the body of the man found in the explosion did not belong to Charles Cutter, but to a detective hired by the research company who was on Cutter's tail. Authorities speculate that Cutter faked his death, absconded with the data and is hiding out in a foreign country.

Sarah tried to steady her breathing as the shock of what she'd read settled in. Dear God, was her father alive? If so, why hadn't Sol told her?

Footsteps sounded on the hardwood entrance and she jerked her head up, shocked to see Sol and Arnold Hughes approaching. Hughes was a tall man with broad shoulders and a wide-set jaw. An air of authority radiated about them that Sarah had always admired and feared at the same time.

The second she saw the frown on Sol's face, though, fear overrode her admiration.

"What are you doing, Sarah?"

She held the article toward him, then signed, "Is it true? Is my father alive?" Her lips quivered as she fought tears. "Did he fake his death?"

Sol and Hughes exchanged concerned looks. Sol pinched the bridge of his nose with his fingers, then shook his head, and sat down, putting his cane aside. An age-spotted hand covered her trembling one. "No, honey, your father is not alive."

"What about this article? The police thought the man's body in the fire belonged to a detective."

"One officer questioned the body, but dental records proved the man was your father. Later, the police verified the findings and closed the case." Sol stacked the scrapbooks. "I should have gotten rid of these a long time ago. I'm going to burn them now."

"No." Sarah caught his arm.

"Sarah, stop it," Sol said in a harsh voice.

Sarah pulled at his hands, releasing him long enough to sign. "Don't, Sol, I need this connection to my past."

"But these books are filled with horrible reminders of what your father did to you and your mother." Sol's eyes softened with worry. "Sarah, it's not healthy for you to obsess over it now."

"I need to know the truth." She turned to Hughes and scribbled on a pad, "Tell me about my father. Sol never wanted to talk about him when I was growing up, but I need to know everything."

"This won't do you any good." Sol gestured toward Hughes. "Please wait in the living room while I talk to her."

"I'm sorry about your father, Sarah." Hughes made a sympathetic sound. "When we first met, he was a good man. But he let greed get to him, and there was nothing we could do." Hughes patted her shoulder, then left the room.

Sarah's throat clogged with emotions. Maybe her father had been a traitor, had been the horrible man they painted him to be, but the reporter's comments about the microbiologist nagged at her. "What about Jerome Simms?"

The vein on the top of Sol's forehead throbbed. "Who?"

"He was a microbiologist who worked at the research center. He supposedly died in a boating accident, but that reporter said his death was suspicious—"

"Why the hell have you been talking to that reporter?"

"I didn't. He called and mentioned to Adam—"

"Adam? So, now you and this detective are on a first-name basis?" Sol paced across the room. "What's gotten into you, Sarah? I've supported you and loved you like you were my own daughter, and now you're trying to ruin the center that I've worked years to create?"

"I'm not," Sarah signed. "But I have to know the truth. I want to help Adam find his sister."

"The truth is that your father was a traitor and a murderer."

Sarah flinched.

"But I tried to cover up for him and spare you some of the painful details, so let it go."

"What about Jerome Simms's death? And Adam's sister—"

"I don't know anything about Black's sister. I was in that room with you for God's sake and I didn't hear a thing!"

"But I did. And I can't help but wonder if one of the scientists she worked with hurt her. Maybe they wanted to steal her research—"

"Do you hear yourself?" Sol bellowed. "Arnold and I handpicked the scientists and companies that have come to the center ourselves. We screen them so we won't have a repeat of what your father did. We're doing good things here, Sarah, research that will make the world a better place, yet you're practically accusing us of the opposite." He ran a hand down his face. "Are you so ungrateful for all I've done that you'd ruin it by all this ridiculous garbage about hearing a woman being abducted?" He hoisted the scrapbooks in his arms and tossed them into the fireplace. When he reached for a match, Sarah grabbed his hands and knocked the matches on the floor.

Anger flared in Sol's eyes, and he drew his hand back and slapped her.

ADAM FORCED HIMSELF to go through the motions as he watched the crime team finish up, but a deep and numbing pain had overcome him. His limbs felt heavy, his chest tight, his stomach queasy.

He had to face the fact that Denise, his little baby sister, the one he'd taught to ride a bike, to kick a soccer ball, might be dead. And the perverted coward who'd probably killed her might have taken her whereabouts to his grave.

While the crime scene guys bagged evidence, he and Clay had searched Gates's desk and his computer for any information that might offer a lead. All of Gates's work files were protected with a password, so he'd already called to see about getting a warrant issued to search them. Of course, he knew CIRP would fight him.

So far, the police found nothing except a few notes declaring how much Gates loved Denise, and some technical information on Alzheimer's.

"Bag these notes," Clay said, handing them to Trantino, one of the crime scene specialists.

"Any news on his family?" Adam asked.

"Father's deceased." Clay answered. "Mother's been notified. She's on her way."

"Did you find anything on his background?"

Clay removed the small notepad from his pocket. "Gates grew up in Atlanta. Attended Emory University, majored in biology. Tried to get into med school but failed."

"Any specific reason?"

"He had the grades, but one of his professors recommended counseling for him—she claimed he kept following her around. Called it creepy."

"She file charges?"

"No, she said he seemed harmless, but he gave her the creeps."

"What happened?"

"New semester began. She figured he moved on."

And when he moved to Savannah, he'd latched on to Denise. Nausea rolled in Adam's stomach. "Any information on hideaway spots the man might use, a beach house or cabin maybe?"

"No, but we'll keep looking."

"Detective Black?" Trantino waved him over. "We're ready to take Gates's body to the morgue."

"Make sure the medical examiner does an autopsy. I want to know what he injected himself with."

The ruddy-faced cop nodded, and gave the go-ahead to remove the body. Adam and Clay followed, led by a group of Seaside Securities officers. As soon as they reached the front double-glass doors, a commotion broke out on the steps outside. Somehow reporters had gotten wind of the murder and crowded the front door, cameras flashing. An elderly lady with red hair ran up the steps, waving her arms hysterically. "Where is my baby boy? Donny, where is he?"

Outside, another team of security guards pushed at the crowd of reporters while one grabbed the woman's arms to hold her back. She sobbed as the paramedics carried the gurney through the throng of people.

Adam's throat ached at the sight before him, his own grief so deep he sympathized with the man's mother. Still, the dead man might have killed his sister.

"Donny! Oh, God, no, no, my baby, God no!"

The guard pulled her away while the paramedics slid Gates's body into the back of the ambulance. Reporters crowded the door, fighting to speak to Bradford. One nearly accosted Adam, another dove for Gates's mother. She threw her hands over her face. "Who hurt my boy! Who killed him?"

Robey Burgess, the reporter who'd written the story about Sarah, shoved a microphone in Adam's face. "Tell us what happened, Detective."

Adam glared at Burgess. "We have no comment. Now, get out of the way or I'll arrest you for obstructing justice."

SARAH'S HAND flew up to cover her stinging jaw, a sob gurgling in her throat. She'd only seen Sol lose his temper a couple of times, but he had never raised a hand to her before.

"Sarah," his voice broke, and he reached for her, regret and anguish in his eyes. "I'm sorry, honey, I—I don't know what came over me."

Sarah moved away from the wall where she'd landed and headed to the door. She had to leave, to get out of there.

Sol caught her arm. "Honey, please don't go like this. We'll sit down and talk, I've been under so much pressure lately, and—"

She jerked away, hurt and betrayal splintering through her. And for the first time, distrust. Sol had tried to protect her all her life, yet had he told her the truth about her father? Could he possibly still be alive?

"I have to go," she signed, tears clogging her eyes.

"But, Sarah—"

"No," she signed. "Maybe we can talk tomorrow or the next day, but right now I need to be alone."

She turned and fled the room as quickly as she could. She had no car, she remembered, thinking of Adam. He would expect her to be here when he returned. The memory of Sol slapping her was too painful, though. She had to leave. She'd take one of Sol's cars and bring it back later.

She found the keys to the Honda she'd driven when she lived with Sol on the brass hook in the kitchen where they always hung. She grabbed them and rushed to the car, fighting the emotions churning through her. She wanted to see Adam, to know if he'd found Denise. To have him hold her and tell her everything was all right.

No, she didn't need Adam Black; she had to depend on herself. And she had to find out if there were more articles about her father being alive, if there was any chance...

Seconds later, she pulled out of the driveway and headed along the coast, hoping to clear her head. The evening spring shower turned into a heavy rain, the water pelting the windshield fogging the visibility. She turned on the wipers and defroster and slowed her speed, startled when the sound of thunder rent the air.

Old childhood memories assaulted her. She hated thunderstorms. The dark rolling clouds that hovered above. The loud booming sounds that tore through the sky. The jagged patches of lightning. The sound of her mother's cries.

Rain slashed against the glass, the wind outside tossed a broken tree limb in the road, and she swerved to avoid it. An oncoming car blew its horn and Sarah jumped, then pulled the Honda back to the road, but bright lights glared at her from behind, almost blinding her. The Bay Bridge was coming up. She squinted and tried to focus as she approached the bridge but suddenly a car slammed into her from behind. Sarah's heart lurched. She hit the brakes, clenching the steering wheel to get control, but the car hydroplaned, spun around, then screeched to a stop, nose-down, hanging over the edge of the embankment.

Chapter Twelve

Rain drizzled down, but Adam shook it off as he approached Donny Gates's mother. Clay's hand on his arm stopped him. "Let me talk to her, Black."

Adam nodded, shoving his hands in the pockets of his jeans as he stepped behind Clay. Clay took an umbrella from one of the paramedics and shielded Mrs. Gates, who seemed oblivious to anything except her son's lifeless body being carried into the ambulance.

"I'm sorry about your son's death." Clay placed a comforting hand on Mrs. Gates. "I hate to ask you this now, but from what we found inside Donny's locker, it appears he was obsessed with the doctor he worked for, Denise Harley. We have reason to believe Donny might have taken her—"

"Taken her?" Mrs. Gates shrieked. "What are you implying?"

Clay cleared his throat. "Dr. Harley has been missing for days, ma'am, and the suicide note your son wrote implied that he might have harmed her."

"No!" The woman swayed, and Clay steadied her.

"I'm sorry, ma'am, but if he was holding her someplace, it's important we find out where. She might still be alive."

"My Donny wouldn't hurt a fly!" Mrs. Gates's eyes went wild with anger. "He's the sweetest, most angelic boy there ever was. And he would never kill himself."

"Did your son own a cabin or have a special place he liked to go to be alone? A boat, maybe?"

"Donny wouldn't hurt that woman!"

"Look, Mrs. Gates," Adam said softly, moving up beside Clay. "Denise Harley is my sister. I know you loved your son, but I love Denise, and I want to find her. If you know anything that can help us, please tell us now."

The paramedic popped his head around the edge of the ambulance. "We're ready to roll."

Adam nodded, aware the thunderstorm was heating up, that every second that passed was precious.

"But I want to go with my Donny," Mrs. Gates shouted.

"We'll get someone to drive you," Clay offered.

Sniffling, she accepted the handkerchief Clay offered and took his hand.

"Please, Mrs. Gates," Adam said, not caring that emotions tinged his voice. "Was there a place?"

"No, I'm— Wait, he did have a boat at one time, but I thought he sold it."

"Where did he keep it?"

She dabbed at her tear-filled eyes again. "Down at the marina. I think he called it *My Fair Lady.*"

Adam palmed his car keys and jogged toward his car, his heart pounding.

THE CAR WAS going into the water. It teetered on the edge, rocking back and forth, the ocean crashing beneath her, the storm raging in its intensity.

Fear closed Sarah's throat, sucking the air from her lungs, and pain knifed through her ankle. Someone had intentionally hit her—someone who wanted to kill her.

The front of the car was smashed in, her foot trapped, while rain slashed the rooftop, mingling with the sounds of thunder. Forcing air through her nose, she fought the panic. She had to think.

She slowly tried to pull her foot free, but the car rocked forward, and she clutched the steering wheel, trying desperately to lean back so the car would level off.

Dear God, she was going to die.

She glanced over the embankment and saw the waves crashing against jagged rocks. How far down was the water? How deep? Several hundred feet, she guessed. If the car crashed, would the impact kill her?

If not, maybe she could climb out the window.

Holding her breath, she pulled her leg again, but her foot was wedged between the brake and the accelerator. A sob of frustration caught in her throat.

Would she die so soon after having her hearing restored? When the world had just opened up to her? Before she experienced love or had a baby?

Before she found out what had happened to Adam's sister? Before she experienced the thrill of lying in a man's arms?

Of lying in Adam Black's arms?

His handsome, anguished face rose in her mind.

She wanted to kiss him just one more time.

Clenching her fists for control, she formed a plan. The car screeched, tires spewing dirt and grass. The wheels slipped, and the sharp sound of the axle grinding splintered the air. She had to do something.

Silently she counted—one, two, three. She reached for the doorhandle, giving her leg a sharp yank at the same time. Her ankle pulled free, but the car pitched forward, and crashed into the rocks.

ADAM FOUGHT through the haze of the downpour, taking the roads way too fast for the weather conditions, his pulse hammering. The marina came into view and Adam cut off the images that flashed into his mind. He wouldn't let himself believe Gates had put Denise's body into the ocean.

Seconds later, Adam spun into the parking lot, water spraying off the car as he screeched to a halt. As soon as he found Denise, he'd call Sarah and see if she was okay.

No, he would take Denise to meet her. Tell his sister that Sarah had helped save her life.

He grabbed a flashlight from beneath the seat of the car, and took off running. A security guard jumped from his station. "Excuse me, sir—"

"SPD, here on official business." Adam flashed his badge and ran past. He heard shouting behind him and recognized Clay's voice as well. Shadows clung to the boats, lightning illuminating the sky and flashing off the ships. He squinted to read the names, searching each slip. *The Honeymooner. Donovan's Dames.* The *Lady Bird. My Fair Lady.*

That was it. A thirty-foot cruiser.

He jumped aboard, searching the dim exterior for any signs of life. "Denise?"

Nothing.

His chest heaving, he pushed at the door, but it was locked. Damn. Not caring about protocol or if he had a search warrant, he took his booted foot and slammed it against the door. It didn't budge. Furious, he kicked it again.

Suddenly Clay was behind him. "Move over, buddy. I got a duplicate key from maintenance."

Damn, he was so panicked he hadn't been thinking.

Then Clay opened the door, and Adam ducked to go inside. Darkness bathed the interior, the scent of cleaning chemicals strong. He inched toward the inside to flip on a light. But the power wasn't connected, so he switched on his flashlight, fanning it across the room to scan the inside. "Denise?"

Nothing.

His pulse tripped into double time. He moved slowly into the cabin, scanning its width. A kitchen area, table, bath to the left. Empty. He crept toward the back while Clay took the side cabin.

The master stateroom held a queen-size bed, but the room was empty.

"There's nobody here," Clay said in a quiet voice as he moved up beside him. "And it doesn't look like anyone has been here for a while."

Adam choked back a reply. Clay was wrong. Someone had been there or else the scent of cleaning supplies wouldn't have been so strong. Which could mean Gates had cleaned up after a crime.

What the hell had he done with Denise?

Chapter Thirteen

Adam and Clay spent the next half hour searching the boat for notes, papers, anything that might give them a clue.

"I don't see any sign that he'd planned to bring her here," Clay said. "Normally these guys stage an elaborate scene to have the place ready."

Adam checked the closets, searching for women's clothing. Clay was right. If Gates had planned to bring Denise here, he would probably have bought her clothes, a nightgown, toiletries, everything to aid in his sick seduction.

But telling himself the empty boat was a good sign didn't alleviate the tightness in Adam's chest. The sound of his cell phone broke into his thoughts. He answered it on the first ring. "Detective Black here."

"Adam, this is Bernstein. We just got a call in that there was an accident over at the Bay Bridge. Car was registered to Sol Santenelli." Bernstein paused for a breath. "I know you've been investigating his goddaughter."

"Yeah? Was Santenelli hurt?"

"No. Santenelli wasn't in the car. Sarah Cutter was driving."

Adam's heart stopped. "Is she all right?"

"Paramedics are with her now."

"I'll be right there."

SARAH CLUTCHED the blanket around her, dizzy with the flashing lights of the ambulance and police cars swirling against the dark sky. Two police officers had arrived to help her, the paramedics on their heels. She shivered as she remembered the fear that had nearly paralyzed her those last few seconds before she'd jumped to safety, and the horrible sound of the car crashing into the rocks below.

She had barely escaped the same fate.

"You have a slight sprain to that ankle," the paramedic said, "but it's not broken. Take it easy for a few days, keep some ice on it so the swelling goes down. You should have it X-rayed, just in case."

Sarah nodded, offering a small smile, as he wrapped her foot.

"Are you hurt anywhere else?"

Sarah shook her head. The paramedic frowned, as if to ask why she wasn't talking, but she gestured that she was deaf. He surprised her by signing, "Tell me if you're hurt anywhere else."

She signed her thanks. "I'm a little bruised from landing on the concrete when I jumped from the car."

The constant throb was making her slightly nauseous, too, the chill from the rain seeping into her, sending shivers up and down her body. Although the rain had stopped, her wet hair lay plastered to her head, her clothes were torn, her knee scraped and bloody. But thank God she was alive.

"The police want to ask you some questions," the paramedic signed.

Sarah nodded again, recognizing the female officer as the one she'd met when she'd first gone to the precinct to tell the police about Denise's abduction. She seemed slightly more approachable now, even concerned, as she knelt beside Sarah. She must have seen the paramedic signing, because she introduced herself and asked him to stay.

"I'm Officer Bernstein. You're all right, Ms. Cutter?"

Sarah nodded, and signed that she was bruised and shaken, but had no life-threatening injuries.

"I know you must be upset." Bernstein said. "I—"

"Sarah."

Sarah jerked her head up at the sound of Adam's familiar gruff voice. Bernstein craned her neck to see him, a smile lifting her lips. "Made it awfully fast, Black."

"I was at the marina."

Sarah ached for him to hold her, but he stood ramrod straight, his jaw tight, countless emotions swirling in his dark gaze that she didn't understand. But the pain that resided in those depths told her he hadn't found his sister.

As if she sensed Sarah wanted to talk to Adam, Officer Bernstein moved aside to speak to another officer.

"What did you find out about Denise?" Sarah asked, letting the paramedic interpret for her.

A second of anguish tightened Adam's jaw, but he swallowed, his voice controlled when he spoke. "Gates is dead. Looks like suicide. He left a note declaring his love for Denise, implying that he might have killed her."

Tears filled Sarah's eyes. She'd tried to hold it together after the accident, had tried to be brave, but seeing the desolation in Adam's expression hammered away the last of her control. Somehow, though irrationally, she felt responsible for not finding Denise in time. Adam knelt, a shaky sigh escaping him, then pulled her into his arms.

Sarah buried herself in his warmth, taking solace in his strong embrace as he crooned comforting words and held her tight.

EMOTIONS CLOGGED Adam's throat as he pulled Sarah tighter against his chest. He might have already lost Denise; he could barely even think of it. He didn't want to lose Sarah, too.

He didn't have time to analyze his feelings or even fight them; but he knew that at that moment he was more connected to her than to any woman he'd ever known, and her silent tears tore into him.

Silent, suffering, brave Sarah.

He shouldn't have left her alone. He wouldn't do so again, not until he'd found the person trying to hurt her and locked him behind bars.

"Are you really all right?" he choked out.

She nodded against his chest, her tears soaking his already damp shirt.

Adam turned to the paramedic with raised brows.

"She has a sprain and some bruises," the young man replied, "but she's going to be fine. She should have that ankle X-rayed."

"All right. We will," Adam assured him. He stroked Sarah's wet hair from her face, cupped her chin in his jerky hands and forced her to look into his eyes. A muscle ticked in his jaw when he noticed the sharp redness to her cheek.

Her trembling started again.

"I'm so sorry, Sarah, you don't deserve all this." Adam gently traced a finger over her swollen cheek. "Do you want me to call your godfather?"

She shook her head no, an odd almost frightened look in her eye. Why wouldn't she want Santenelli to know she'd been in an accident?

He pressed a gentle kiss to her temple. "Tell me everything that happened."

She pulled away from him slightly and signed, letting the paramedic interpret for her again, relaying the details of the accident.

Adam's face blanched. "Someone intentionally forced you off the road?"

She nodded, her bottom lip quivering.

"Did you see what kind of car hit you?"

"No, it was dark and the storm was raging around me."

"I don't understand," Adam said, questions racing through his head. "We thought the person tried to hurt you because of Denise. But if Gates kidnapped Denise, and he's dead, we must be wrong."

Unless Gates hadn't kidnapped his sister, Adam thought, silently. Or unless someone wanted Sarah dead and it had nothing to do with Denise.

IT SEEMED LIKE HOURS later when they finished with X rays and Adam drove her home from the hospital. Sarah huddled inside the blanket. She couldn't get warm, couldn't relax, couldn't forget that she and Sol had fought. That she had seen the article about her father possibly being alive. That she had almost died.

And that Adam thought Denise might already be dead at the hands of Donny Gates.

Adam's questions tumbled through her mind. If Gates had kidnapped Denise and killed himself, who had followed her and caused her to crash? And why? With Denise's death being blamed on Donny, all the questions about Adam's sister would be put to rest.

It didn't make sense.

She stole a look at Adam and shivered, a cold engulfing her from the inside out. He looked as if he were barely holding himself together. His hands were clenched around the steering wheel, his shoulders stiff, his eyes glued to the road. He must be hurting so much inside. She ached for him, and desperately wanted to make everything all right.

But then there was Sol. She hadn't told Adam about the article suggesting her father might still be alive. Although Sol had denied it, she had to find out if there had been any reason to think her father might have survived the fire.

But if he had, wouldn't the police or the FBI have gone after him?

So what had upset her godfather so badly? She'd never seen him lose his temper before like that, especially at her. He'd always been so loving, her Rock of Gibraltar.

But her rock had crumbled, and she didn't know if she would ever feel the same about him again.

Adam's hands shook so badly he didn't know if he could make it to Sarah's. The day had been too much. The revelations about Gates, finding those pictures, discovering Gates dead, then not finding Denise. And Sarah's accident.

She could have died.

His chest constricted, the air caught in his lungs, and suddenly he couldn't breathe. Feeling out of control, he slowed the car and pulled into a picnic area overlooking the ocean and forced himself to do some breathing exercises.

Sarah stirred and opened her sleepy bedroom eyes. The rain had finally slacked off, and a sliver of the moon peeked from behind the black clouds, illuminating the red bruise on her cheek. She looked so pale and fragile, yet she was so tough. She'd put herself in danger to help him and Denise.

He couldn't fight his need any longer. He dragged her into his arms and kissed her, forgetting all about her innocence as he sated himself with her sweet, tantalizing taste. A mixture of Earl Grey tea, heat and passion.

Her lips felt supple beneath his, her soft sigh of surrender a plea for more. Like a starving man, he had to touch her. His hands skated along her neck, then skimmed down her back, pulling her tightly into the hard planes of his body. She felt soft and filled him with a headiness he'd never felt before. She threaded her fingers in the sides of his hair, responding with a fiery hunger that sent his senses spinning. His sex stirred and swelled as he cupped her breasts. Her chest heaved with a shaky breath, and he drove his tongue inside her mouth, tracing a finger over her tight nipple. The ocean crashed in the background and the whisper of night sounds played music around them, her raspy breath like a lover's caress.

Dropping kisses along her neck, he slipped his hand beneath her shirt, groaning when his palm brushed warm skin. Then he was pulling at her bra, tearing away the cups so his hands could fit over her bare breast. The soft whimper she emitted nearly undid him.

He wanted to hear her call his name.

The realization that she couldn't jolted him back to reality. To the fact that Sarah was vulnerable and needed things he could never give her. Like a tender man, not one driven by lust and rough emotions, not one constantly surrounded by danger. She needed marriage and children. The kind of life he'd given up on a long time ago. The kind of life he didn't deserve, not after letting Pamela die.

Still, he wanted her so badly he could barely help himself. And he cared for her more than he could ever tell her.

"God, Sarah, I'm sorry. I don't know what came over me."

She clutched his arms and tried to force him to meet her gaze, but he shook his head. "Don't. I shouldn't have mauled you like that. For God's sake, someone just tried to kill you."

His harsh words snapped her out of the sensual haze surrounding them, and she stiffened. Without another word, he righted her clothes, pulled back onto the street and drove in silence the rest of the way home.

Chapter Fourteen

The minute Adam helped Sarah into her house, the phone trilled. Adam watched, letting the answering machine kick on.

"Sarah, listen this is Sol. I'm—" he hesitated, his voice cracking "—I'm sorry about earlier. I don't know what came over me. I've been under a lot of stress with the center, and I thought we got past this thing with your dad a long time ago." He cleared his throat. "I guess I thought that after all these years, you considered me your father, and...well, I'm sorry I lost my temper. Please call me, honey. I love you."

The phone clicked into silence. Sarah looked shaken. Adam coaxed her to sit down and take the weight off her injured ankle.

"What was he talking about, Sarah?"

She shrugged, not meeting his eyes.

He lifted her chin with his thumb, his gut clenching at the raw emotions swirling in her expression. Because of their heated kiss or her godfather? "Tell me what happened. When I left you at Santenelli's, I thought you planned to stay there."

She tapped her fingernails on her leg for a moment,

then picked up a pad and wrote, ''I was, but Sol and I got into an argument.''

''About what?''

She sighed. ''I was asking questions about my dad. He didn't want to talk about it.''

''Then what?''

''I wanted to keep the scrapbooks he had, he wanted to burn them. We argued and he—''

''He what?''

''He hit me,'' Sarah finished.

Anger blazed inside Adam, swift and hard. His hand rose to her cheek, the barest touch of his fingertip grazing the tender spot. ''Is that how you got this bruise?''

Sarah nodded, still not meeting his gaze.

Her godfather was the one person she trusted and loved, yet he'd hurt her.

Trembling with the power of his emotions, Adam took a deep breath. ''Is that why you borrowed his car and drove off?''

She nodded again, hugging her arms around her waist.

He wanted to touch her again so badly he had to fist his hands by his sides. If he did touch her, it would be a repeat of what happened in the car. He'd be helpless to control his hunger.

So he didn't touch her. He simply whispered her name. ''Sarah.''

She finally looked into his eyes.

''Has your godfather ever hit you before?''

She shook her head no, and relief surged through him. The shock of the evening was wearing on her, though. Her face looked pale, her vibrant blue eyes dull. "Why don't you take a warm bath? I'll fix us something to eat."

She tried to stand, wincing when she put weight on her sore ankle, so he picked her up, then headed to the bathroom. He helped her sit down on the toilet, then turned the hot water on and added bubble bath to the steamy water.

"I'm sorry about your godfather," he said quietly.

She shrugged, lifted her chin in defiance as if to say it didn't matter.

But it did.

He saw the anguish in the way she stiffened.

Only he had no idea how to help her.

SARAH SLOWLY undressed, the stiffness in her body a testament to her earlier fall. The day had been hell.

But Adam's kiss had been heaven.

Why had he stopped? And why did he think it was a mistake?

Granted she was innocent, but she'd had the powerful urge to throw herself into his arms again and beg him to make love to her.

He obviously found her lacking.

She couldn't allow herself to lean on him again. She had taken care of herself for a long time. She would go on doing so when Adam walked out of her life.

After all, if she needed anything, Sol was always there for her. Or at least he had been in the past. But would she feel comfortable going to him after what had happened between them today?

Could her father truly be alive?

She slipped on a robe, tiptoed over to her laptop and pulled up all the stories she could find on her father and the company. But a half hour later, she'd discovered nothing to suggest he might have survived.

Exhausted, she pinned her hair on top of her head, reheated the water and sank into the warm soapy water in the bathtub.

Her muscles protested, the strain of the day wearing on her physically and emotionally. Closing her eyes, she forced her breathing to slow, but the day's events refused to leave her in peace.

Images of the fire that had killed her mother and almost taken her own life worked their way into her subconscious.

She was five years old again, lying on the couch taking a nap when the first sound of the explosion hit. A storm was brewing outside, thunder and lightning heating up the sky. She'd thought the sound had been thunder. She tried to run to her mother.

"Get out! Run!" her mother screamed.

But Sarah couldn't, not without her mother. Then another explosion rent the air and flames burst all around her. Sarah's mother appeared in the doorway, flames eating at her. Sarah screamed and ran toward her. But her mother pushed her away and Sarah cried out.

"Run, Sarah, run!"

Sarah panicked and tripped. Flames licked at her as she sprawled on the floor. Terrified, she searched for her daddy. She saw him outside the window looking in.

Yes, her father would save them.

Then pain slammed into her head, and she fell into silence. A cold, deafening, lonely, terrifying silence.

Blackness swirled around her. Then she was wak-

ing up in the hospital. She couldn't hear. She couldn't talk.

"Your mommy and daddy are gone," Sol had whispered.

She couldn't hear his voice, but she saw the tears in his eyes and she knew her parents were dead.

No, she cried silently. It couldn't be true. She had screamed out for her daddy to save them.

And then a few months later, someone told her that her father had set the explosion....

FRUSTRATED, Adam scrounged through Sarah's cabinets and the refrigerator, searching for something to make a late-night supper for her. He wasn't hungry himself.

At least not for food.

He wanted Sarah.

Knowing she was lying naked in a bubble bath next door only added torture to his already pounding need. He imagined the water lapping at her breasts, touching her soft round flesh the way his hands itched to. He could see her long slender legs stretched out in the tub, bubbles dotting her calves, her thighs, the water kissing her bare belly, her navel, then lower....

Cursing his wandering libido, he forced himself to block out the images. His hunger for food could be abated. But his hunger for Sarah would have to go unfulfilled.

A quick survey of her cozy kitchen, the bright yellow-and-blue colors, the ceramic calico kittens she collected, the cheery wallpaper and the cozy den with its throw rugs and antiques, only made him think of Sarah more. Sarah Cutter spelled *home*—the cozy kind of home a normal family would have. The kind he'd had before his parents had died. Before he'd become a cop and learned how hard it was to support a family. Sarah was accustomed to nice things, things he'd never be able to give her.

He'd seen the vermin on the streets, and he'd pledged his life to deal with them. No, his lifestyle had nothing to do with home and hearth and raising kids.

That last night with his parents rose to taunt him. His dad hadn't made much money, but he'd always made time for Adam. He'd thrown the ball with him at night, come to all his baseball games, built model cars with him. But his parents' lives had been cut short by a drunk driver. The police had bungled the case, though, and the man had gotten away—the reason Adam had gone into police work. He'd sworn to avenge their deaths by being a good cop, by protecting other innocent people. Especially his sister. But he'd failed her.

He opened the wine and poured two glasses. He and Sarah both deserved a drink to settle their nerves. So, why did he ache for Sarah so much? She was nothing like the no-strings women he usually dated.

Whatever the reason, his hunger raged inside him like an uncontrollable beast. And his feelings for her increased by the minute. But he would not take Sarah. He was in control. Adam Black, detective, desperado, always in control.

A soft cry invaded his thoughts.

He hesitated, one hand on a container of something that appeared to be homemade soup, the other a loaf of French bread. What was that noise? Sarah's cat?

No, Tigger lay curled up on the overstuffed armchair in the corner of the den. The cries grew louder, heart-wrenching in their intensity. The sound drifted from the bathroom. Sarah.

He sipped the wine, struggling over whether to go to her or to let her vent her emotions in private, the way he suspected she'd meant to do.

Only his gut was being torn in two.

He sipped the wine again, opened the container of soup and zapped it in the microwave. Her cries continued to haunt him. She would never ask for help, he realized, because he'd pushed her away.

Fisting his hands, he found himself at the bathroom door. He knocked gently, and waited, but she didn't reply. Right or wrong, he couldn't stop himself; he slipped inside.

She lay back in a sea of bubbles, her beautiful dark hair piled on top of her head, her face dropped forward in her hands, her body trembling with soft silent sobs.

He moved on autopilot, not questioning what he should do. He grabbed the big bath towel, pulled her up to stand, wrapped it around her and carried her to bed.

EMBARRASSED THAT Adam had seen her crying, and hating that she'd lost control, she pulled back. But Adam tunneled his fingers through her hair and held her tightly. She was naked and exposed, both physically and emotionally, she thought, willing herself to be strong. But Adam whispered her name, and she lost all willpower. She buried her head in his shoulder.

"Shh, it's all right."

She'd had a rough day, she reminded herself, one

hand brushing at her tears while the other tugged the towel around her damp breasts.

But so had Adam.

Compassion for him filled her. He was so gentle and tender, yet he'd taken care of her when he must be hurting inside so much himself.

She forgot her embarrassment at the look of tenderness on his face as he laid her on the cool lavender sheets. She tentatively reached up to press a hand against his cheek. Instead of sadness though, heat flared in his eyes.

On a very primal level, Adam wanted her, she realized. She saw the hunger and need, heard the burning rasp of passion in his breath, and felt the evidence of his arousal pulse against her thigh.

He wouldn't act on it, though. He reached for the covers to tuck her in, his expression guarded as if allowing himself the comfort of her arms would make him appear weak. She understood about feeling weak and exposed and out of control.

He didn't deserve to hurt alone, to have no one to hold him and offer him strength. Her comforting body was one thing she could offer.

"Are you hungry or do you want to just rest?" he asked in a gruff voice.

She twined her fingers in his and urged him down beside her. Then she told him with her eyes that she was hungry, but not for food.

For him.

Chapter Fifteen

Sarah flicked the lamp off, so only the soft touch of moonlight spilling through the window illuminated them. She reached up to unbutton the top of his shirt, but Adam caught her hand in his and pressed it to his thigh.

"Sarah, no." He brushed a gentle kiss in her hair, then murmured against her neck, "I'm not the right kind of man for you, my job's made me hard—"

She pressed her finger to his lips to silence him, then lifted his hand and placed it on her breast. He might think he wasn't right for her, but she heard no evil in his whispered warning, only the seductive sound of his beautiful voice. A sound that would erase the harsh reality of the ugly sounds she'd heard earlier today, the sounds of death and anguish, and her own heart beat thrown off-kilter with fear.

He searched her face, the heat from his body radiating around her, his broad jaw clenched as if he were fighting for control. Her heart pounded beneath his fingertips as she gently dropped the towel, exposing her naked breasts. She didn't fear him, and she wanted him to know it.

His breath rasped out, his eyes darkened to an inky

hue and a low guttural moan of acquiescence tore from him, the sound all primal male need.

Heat seared through her as he picked the pins from her hair, dropping them on the floor and finger-combing her long hair down her back while his other hand tormented her breast. Then his lips were everywhere, kissing her mouth, nibbling her neck, dropping featherlight kisses down her throat and into the sensitive hollow of her neck. She ran her hand through his hair, then down his chest, savoring every hard muscle as her fingers caressed him. He licked her mouth with his tongue until she parted her lips and invited him inside.

She wanted him inside her forever.

He exuded power and strength and sex appeal, yet had a tenderness that told her he would never hurt her. At least not physically.

She had to guard her heart, though.

But this time wasn't about heart or soul, it was about living. About taking away the pain and sadness, making the moment magical for both of them. She met each stroke of his tongue with her own, matching his passion with her own swift, potent desire. He tore his mouth from her long enough to yank his shirt off, and toss it to the floor. Hunger pooled low in her belly at the sight of his wide, dark chest. She lifted a finger and flicked her nail across one taut nipple, surprised when he sucked in a sharp breath.

Her gaze met his and a masculine growl of pleasure erupted from him. Feeling powerful now, she tasted him with her tongue, and reveled in the touch of his body growing harder against her thigh. He tore the towel from the rest of her body, covered her smooth legs with his thick muscular ones, his foot brushing her leg in a rhythm that made her ache all over. She clutched his shoulders, parting her legs as he settled between her thighs. His jeans rasped against her flesh, and she silently begged for him to remove them, but he left them on, torturing her by forcing her to wait. Then his mouth covered her nipple, and he licked and gently bit the tip, finally drawing it in his mouth and suckling.

Sarah arched up from the bed, the frenzy of emotions and sensations darting through her almost unbearable. Both pain and pleasure. She had to have more.

He suckled harder, moving to the other breast to love her the same, then lower. Lower he kissed, her navel, the insides of her thighs, then he brushed his mouth across her soft mound and she bucked, whimpering her pleasure.

His breath felt hot, his tongue moist as he teased her heat and drove her wild. Just when she thought she would die from the pleasure, he rose above her, and quickly shucked his jeans and briefs. His sex bulged with his need, and for a brief second, she felt a burst of panic at his size. But this was Adam and her body screamed for him to fill her, to claim her as his, so she spread her legs, traced a finger over the end of his shaft and begged him to join her.

Adam was out of control. He wanted to take Sarah fast and hard, to ride her like she was his forevermore. She was so sensuous and responsive, so passionate and beautiful that his breath tore from his chest in a gut-wrenching moan. But he saw that moment of fear in her eyes, that moment of concern that he might hurt her.

He had to rein in his wildness, slow down this frantic pace, and give her the tender lovemaking she deserved.

So, instead of thrusting inside her until she could feel nothing but him, he slowed his movements, lowered his mouth again and began to gently drive her wild with his tongue. First her breasts again, licking the rosy tips, suckling until she writhed beneath him. Then her honeyed sweetness. She tasted like innocence and woman, like she'd been created to fuel his hunger, her whimpers of pleasure nearly sending him over the edge.

Her blue eyes darkened, turned luminous with passion as she clawed at the sheets, pulling them into her fists as he tortured her over and over. When he felt the tremors of release building within her, he gently pushed her legs wider apart and hungrily devoured her.

Finally, when she arched her body, silently begging him for more, he rose above her, quickly rolled on protection and claimed her as his.

Sensation after sensation rolled through Sarah, each one more heady than the last. She had never dreamed a man's mouth could feel so wonderful, that she would be able to give herself to her lover with such abandon, but being so intimate with Adam somehow seemed right.

He held her gaze as he slowly pushed inside her, pausing to let her body become accustomed to him. But Sarah was riding the wave and wanted him harder, faster.

She didn't want him to hold back. But she sensed that was what he was doing.

She pulled his mouth down to hers, kissed him greedily, not caring that she was clawing at his back.

Finally he moved within her. Not the wild abandon she'd expected from a powerful man like Adam, but a slow, rhythmic rocking motion that tortured her senses. She nuzzled her face in his chest, teasing his nipple with her tongue and raking her hands across his backside. His muscles clenched, he began to move faster, pulling her hips into his. Deeper, deeper, penetrating her, thrusting his thick shaft to her core, forcing her to open wider and give herself to him again. She was coming in a kaleidoscope of colors...

"Oh, Sarah," he groaned. "You feel so good, I can't wait."

A satisfied smile tipped her lips and she thrust against him, almost crying out when she felt him lose control and join her in oblivion.

Seconds later, she drifted to sleep, but the sound of a woman's crying jarred her awake. And she lay in bed and realized that the voices had returned.

Denise.

How was it possible she was hearing them again?

ADAM THOUGHT Sarah had fallen asleep, and knew he had to pull away. His heart tugged painfully as he remembered the emotions gripping him when they'd made love.

Dammit, he never let his feelings get involved.

He slowly regulated his breathing and rolled off her, determined to put some distance between them before he completely lost his objectivity.

"I'll be right back." He hurried to the bathroom, disposed of the protection he was so grateful he'd had, then stared at himself in the mirror. He looked haggard and scruffy and too damn rough for a woman like Sarah.

What the hell had he done?

Knowing he had to talk to her, he splashed water on his face, dried it, then sauntered back to the bed. She was lying sideways wearing nothing but that locket, a sexy smile and the scent of his lovemaking.

He had to say something, but for the life of him, he couldn't speak. She was so damn beautiful. And trusting and sweet. And such a fighter.

She had so much passion inside her.

Sarah held her hand out to him, inviting him back inside her bed, but he saw her troubled expression—was she already having regrets? Then she handed him a note and he squinted, his heart pounding when he read the words, "I heard the voices again, Adam. I don't think we should give up on finding Denise."

ADAM HAD FINALLY fallen asleep, Sarah thought, but Denise's cry disturbed her.

How was it possible? Why would she still have delayed hearing about that night when the rest of her hearing abilities had evened out?

Exhausted, she snuggled into the haven of Adam's arms, sated and happy and fighting regrets. Regrets that she might have given Adam more than her body the night before.

Regrets that she was falling in love with him.

He held her in spoon fashion, his breath whispering against her neck. A strand of his hair tickled her earlobe. But she didn't want to move for fear he'd withdraw from her forever, that he'd tell her it had all been a mistake.

His sex surged against her backside and she wiggled, renewed hunger spiraling through her. But her ankle throbbed, a reminder of the ugly events of the day before.

His hand drifted up her belly and covered her breasts, and she forgot all her ailments. Would he make love to her again this morning? Tender as she was, she wasn't sure she could accept him, but as he pushed his body closer to hers, winding his muscular leg over hers, she realized she'd always be able to make love with Adam.

His sex pulsed and thickened. But suddenly he pulled away from her and she clenched the sheets in her fist, feeling lost and confused.

ADAM COULD EXCUSE himself for the night before. They'd both been shaken by the day—his sister, Donny Gates, her godfather, her accident—but this morning with bright sunlight beaming through the window, the reality of the bruises on her body and danger on her tail, how could he justify taking advantage of her?

And how could she have heard Denise?

He glanced down at her, wondering how it was possible, but all he could think about was the night before. He had taken advantage of her. He couldn't kid himself. She was an innocent, for God's sake. He would walk away with little emotional scarring when this whole thing was over, but she would...would what? Would Sarah want more from him?

Was she falling in love with him?

Hell, maybe he was the fool here—he was no catch and he knew it, and she certainly hadn't mentioned any feelings. Of course, she didn't talk to him at all.

Except they'd communicated last night just fine. He'd heard the desire, the hunger in her body. That was all he'd been looking for. Comfort. Because he'd thought Denise might be dead.

Only he had let feelings seep in.

She turned in his arms, tracing a finger along his jaw and he tensed. Today he had a job to do.

"Sarah, we can't do this again."

Her smile faded, questions in her eyes.

He couldn't look at her lying naked in his arms and not have her again. He swung his legs to the side, bracing his hands on his thighs as he stared at the floor. At the wet towel she'd stripped off, at her lacy panties that had dropped on top of his shoe.

Her hand brushed his back and he fisted his hands around the edge of the bed. "I told you last night I'm not right for you. I don't want you to get the wrong idea here."

The bed shifted as Sarah got up, but Adam's cell phone rang, interrupting them, and he grabbed and answered it.

"Adam?"

"Yeah?"

"This is Russell."

"Did you hear about Gates?" Adam asked.

"Yeah, when I went into work today."

"I'm sorry, I should have told you, but—"

"Forget it. I heard something at work." Russell paused. "I thought it might be important. And it made me wonder if Gates kidnapped Denise."

Adam ran a hand through his hair, catching Sarah's silhouette as she slipped on a robe. Damn, he would miss that sexy body. She hobbled over to the chaise in the corner and sat down, belting the robe, studying him.

"Black, are you listening?" Russell asked, sounding agitated.

"Yeah." He wanted to believe Russell was right. "What is it?"

"The thing with Gates opened up a lot of gossip around the research center. One of the scientists mentioned that Denise was about to reveal a major finding in her research."

"Really?"

"Yeah, and get this. A German pharmaceutical company is flying in three days from now for a meeting about some new discovery CIRP will unveil. Rumor has it that two other companies are close to the same findings, so timing is important. The discovery may sell for millions."

Questions spun in Adam's mind. "Are you suggesting that someone from the center kidnapped Denise and stole her research to sell to this company?"

"I've heard of that stuff happening, haven't you?"

"Yeah." Especially if it involved big money.

"Or someone from the German company might have kidnapped her, forced her to turn over her results to them before a competitor could make an offer or another researcher disclosed the findings."

"That's possible, too." Adam swallowed, bile rising in his throat. "Our only hope is that the research was incomplete, so they have to keep her alive long enough to finish it before they sell."

Chapter Sixteen

Sarah realized Adam had pulled away from her emotionally the minute he had left her bed. She had no idea what to do about it, either. Maybe circumstances and danger had brought them together, but she sensed there could be a lot more to their relationship if he would give them a chance. But if she came across as needy, she would certainly push him away.

The timbre of his voice grew stronger as the conversation continued.

Did he have good news about Denise? A lead?

"Can you let me in Denise's office today and get me access to her files?"

Sarah couldn't hear the caller's response, but seconds later, Adam agreed to meet him before lunch.

He hung up, squaring his shoulders as he turned to her. His naked body was a masterpiece of hard planes and muscles. She wanted him again so badly she ached.

"Mind if I use your shower?"

She shook her head, wondering if he would invite her to join him, hoping he would. She needed the closeness again and sensed he did, too.

Instead he gathered his clothes and explained about

the phone call. "I have to check out Denise's research. If she was on the verge of revealing her findings and a German company planned to buy it, the research center stood to make a small fortune. There's also the chance a competitor wanted the research and kidnapped her to keep her from selling it to the Germans. I'll have Clay check out the company and any competitors working on similar research."

Sarah nodded, toying with her locket while he phoned Clay. If someone from the center was involved, could Sol know something about it?

ADAM KNEW he should finish the discussion with Sarah about their personal relationship, but his sister's life was at stake, and this new information gave him a new angle to explore. Everything else would have to wait.

"I'm going to check into that microbiologist's death this morning, then go to the research facility to meet Russell around eleven." He stalked toward the bathroom. "I want you to go with me, Sarah."

She frowned, but he didn't intend to argue. He wanted her safe, and he didn't trust anyone else to take care of her but him.

A few minutes later, after he'd showered, Sarah surprised him with a hot breakfast. It had been a long time since anyone had taken care of him. The whole scene felt oddly domestic and homey.

He couldn't get used to it.

He ate the eggs and bacon while he booted up the computer. Sarah seemed to have accepted him in his business mode and disappeared into the bathroom to shower. The sound of the water running drove him crazy. He remembered finding her in the tub the night before, her pale skin warm and slippery with bubble bath, moonlight glowing on her naked body, her arms reaching for him, inviting him to be her lover.

Her first lover. Maybe her only one.

No, he couldn't let himself imagine the pleasure of a long-term relationship with her.

Reminding himself about Pamela's death, he forced the images out of his mind and accessed articles about the microbiologist, Jerome Simms. He'd come to work for CIRP right after graduating from Stanford. For two years, he'd worked almost in seclusion at a lab on Nighthawk Island. Some of his studies involved radioactive isotopes, requiring high-tech security and stringent decontamination procedures.

Questions had popped up about his death that had never been answered. The man was an avid swimmer and diver, so why had he drowned? Why had he been boating alone? Supposedly, a storm had risen, but an experienced boater like Simms wouldn't have chanced going out in bad weather. And if he had, he would have known how to handle the crisis.

Next, Adam accessed the research center's history, including major announcements regarding research and new products as well as two competitors working on similar areas.

Information spooled onto the computer screen, dates and names of the scientists involved over the years. He scrolled through the list, pausing when he found an announcement about a new synthetic compound being released that had sold for a huge amount. The announcement had come one week after Simms's accident. Just as Robey Burgess claimed.

Was Denise's research worth killing over? Worry pulled at him. Sarah's godfather had helped start the foundation—could he know something or be involved? If so, she would be devastated. And Adam would have to expose the company, including her godfather.

He phoned Clay and updated him. "Check on any competitors researching Alzheimer's."

"All right," Clay agreed. "The lab came back on that drug Gates used to kill himself—it was insulin."

Adam sighed in frustration. "Hell, anybody could get ahold of that."

The bedroom door opened and Sarah emerged, looking beautiful in a dark-blue blouse and jeans. He was hanging up the phone when she limped toward him, the hint of pain in her eyes hitting him in the gut. Adam couldn't change what had happened yesterday, but he could keep himself from repeating the mistake. Unfortunately, if he found out something to implicate her godfather's involvement, she would be hurt even more.

Sarah returned to the table beside him with the morning paper. Her eyes widened when she opened it. Then she thrust it at him. His pulse hammered at the headline.

"Scandal at CIRP." The article speculated on Gates's obsession with Adam's sister, mentioned the suicide note and the fact that Denise was missing, then implied that Gates had killed her because she'd rejected him.

"Damn," Adam mumbled.

Sarah squeezed his hand, shaken by the story. The last paragraph summarized her godfather's plans for the center and named a few investors. She gestured toward the computer, and Adam explained briefly what he'd learned.

She tilted her Palm Pilot toward him. "You think someone at the research center might have killed Denise and Donny to get Denise's research?"

"It's possible. If not, maybe a competitor did."

"But why kill Donny Gates?"

Adam drummed his fingers on the table. "I don't know. Maybe he really did have an obsession with Denise, or…maybe someone framed him."

"Someone would really do that?"

"Money can be a powerful motivator." Adam shrugged. "If someone was looking for a scapegoat and they knew Gates had a thing for Denise, they might have used him. Maybe Gates even discovered their plans for Denise, so they had to silence him."

But if Denise's research was incomplete, they might keep her alive to finish it. If so, and the German company planned to meet with them in three days, time was running out. Once they had the research in their hands, the kidnapper would have no reason to keep Denise alive.

SARAH STARED OUT the window, watching the landscape pass in a blur as they drove to the research center on Catcall Island. She couldn't believe someone at the center would harm Adam's sister for her work. But if they had, her godfather Sol couldn't have known about it. Could he? No, not Sol.

Sol would never do anything illegal—he'd despised her father for betraying them all and had worried Sarah's father's reputation might affect the center when they first opened. Surprisingly, the scientific community admired Santenelli for taking in the traitor's daughter.

Her hand rose to touch the bruise on her cheek

where he had hit her, her mind spinning. If Sol knew someone was trying to hurt her, he'd stop them. He loved her like she was his own daughter…didn't he?

She'd been driving Sol's car, so the person who'd run her off the road might have been trying to hurt Sol.

Dear God, she hadn't thought of that before. Maybe Sol had uncovered something about Denise's disappearance and the person had really meant to kill Sol.

She should tell Adam.

No, she was simply panicking. Adam would find out the truth.

A few minutes later, Russell Harley escorted them through security. Sarah's ankle ached, but she ignored the pain, not willing to lean on Adam today. Not after the way he'd pushed her away.

ADAM HATED SEEING the pain in Sarah's eyes as she struggled to walk through the center—he knew she'd refused his help because of what had happened between them. But it was better this way, he reminded himself, because he couldn't let himself be distracted. He had to find Denise.

"This is my office." Russell led them through a set of metal doors that closed behind them like elevator doors. They had come through the lab, a basic research facility with sterile stainless-steel counters, microscopes and some high-tech instruments Russell had briefly explained. Various chemical smells permeated the room. Russell's office, which adjoined the lab, consisted of a plain desk piled high with research notes, books jammed haphazardly into a wall bookcase and diagrams of molecular structures on the walls. "You can use my computer to access Denise's research. I know Denise's password. I'll get you into her files.''

The computer keys clicked away as Russell retrieved the data. Several minutes later, Adam stared at copies of his sister's notes.

''She was methodical,'' Russell said, a smile on his mouth. ''Her attention to detail was one of the things I admired most about her.''

Adam nodded, thinking how he hadn't trusted Russell when he'd first called. He'd even wondered if Russell was setting him up. But judging from the concern on his face, Russell must still love Denise. Otherwise, he wouldn't endanger himself by sneaking into her files. Unless…he'd altered them?

''Explain these.'' Adam pointed to the chemical notations.

Sarah read over his shoulder while Russell skimmed the summary of the various studies. ''Denise was researching a new compound to be given to pregnant women to enhance cognitive growth and prevent mental retardation in high-risk babies at the fetal stage.''

''Whew, impressive,'' Adam mumbled. ''But Bradford lied when he said Denise was working on Alzheimer's research.''

Sarah squeezed his shoulder and smiled in agreement.

Russell pulled at his chin. ''Probably because this project was highly controversial.''

''You mean if it fell into the wrong hands, some people might try to use it to alter the genes of healthy babies.''

''There's been talk about creating the perfect child.''

This was definitely monumental, Adam realized, a feeling of trepidation sinking in. The kind of thing dozens of companies and countries might want.

"According to Denise's notes, she had one last study, and she was waiting on FDA approval before she could go into clinical trials."

"Would a company be interested in the product before clinical trials?"

"Sure." Russell removed his glasses and pinched the bridge of his nose. "Foreign governments don't have the same requirements as the U.S."

"So, this German company could be interested in Denise's research?"

"It's possible." Russell shrugged. "Of course, there's at least a hundred other projects here they might be coming to talk with CIRP about."

Too coincidental. And Adam hated coincidences.

Sarah pushed a pad of paper toward him with a hastily scribbled question. "If she hadn't completed the study, could they have taken her somewhere to finish it?"

Adam chewed the inside of his cheek. "It's possible."

Of course, he still didn't know who had kidnapped her—the Germans? A competitor? One of the scientists at CIRP who was jealous of her work or had gotten greedy? And if it was a co-worker at CIRP, did the center know about the person's intentions?

"I HAVE TO TALK to Bradford," Adam said.

Russell led the way. "I'd like to hear what he has to say, too."

Adam placed a hand on Russell's chest. "No, Harley, I think it would be better if you stayed out of it."

Russell exhaled, worry knitting his brow. "I still care about Denise, Adam. I want to help find her."

"You already have helped. But the less involved you appear, the safer it will be for you." Russell started to argue, but Adam cut him off. "Just keep your eyes and ears open and let me know if you hear anything else."

Russell agreed and Sarah followed Adam to the neighboring building housing Bradford's office.

The burly man didn't appear happy to see them, but he gestured for them to take a seat, then propped himself on the desk edge, his arms folded. "I'm sorry about Denise's death. She was a top-notch researcher."

Adam clenched his hands on his knees. "Why do you say she's dead?"

Bradford shifted, putting his weight on his other foot. "I read in the paper that her assistant committed suicide, that he left a note saying he killed her."

"He implied it but he never admitted it," Adam said. "I have reason to believe she's still alive."

Shock ruddied his features. "But—"

"But what?" Adam's temper flared. "I know about the big German company coming in three days, to make a deal. I also know that a week after Jerome Simms died, the center announced a big sale."

Bradford nervously replied. "That's just a coincidence."

"Listen, Doctor," Adam snarled, "I deal with the law, and that's too much coincidence for me."

"All right." Bradford wiped his forehead with a monogrammed handkerchief. "I'll tell you the truth, but you're not going to like it."

Adam gritted his teeth, stepped back from the man

and watched him fall backward into his chair. Bradford took several seconds to calm himself.

"Spill it, Bradford. Do you know where Denise is?"

"No." Bradford held up a hand when Adam started to pounce again. "We think she may have run off with the research."

"What? You didn't mention this earlier?"

"We were trying to protect her reputation and ours, in case we were mistaken." Bradford sighed. "And we didn't want to create a panic with a potential investor coming in."

"My sister wouldn't steal research. Besides, I just saw her files."

A vein pulsed in Bradford's pale forehead, looking as if it might explode. "Who gave you access—"

"Forget who gave me access, her research was there."

"Not all of it," Bradford said, his voice lethal. "The files she left are incomplete, but Denise had finished the research. We suspect she took the research to another company to sell it herself."

Chapter Seventeen

The scenario sounded vaguely familiar, Sarah thought, thinking of the accusations against her father, the ones she'd never thought to question before. Now, she had all kinds of questions.

"My sister did no such thing," Adam said in a dark voice. "Denise was…is one of the most dedicated doctors you have. She wouldn't betray her company, much less sell important research to a competitor without CIRP's approval. She'd be afraid it might fall into the wrong hands."

Bradford planted both hands on his desk. "I told you our suspicions. But with Gates's suicide, we wondered if he killed her and dumped her body in the ocean." A long weary sigh rattled out. "Unfortunately, if he did, we'll never find her or her research."

Sarah shuddered at the vivid images his words evoked.

"If Denise's discovery is incomplete, why are the Germans coming here in three days to buy it?"

"They aren't. They're here about another project."

"What project?"

"That's confidential, Detective Black. I'm not about to expose it and risk losing the deal for the center.'' He crossed his arms, his lips tight. ''But I can assure you it has nothing to do with your sister's work.''

''I don't believe you,'' Adam said. ''But I will find out the truth, Bradford. And so help me, if you've hurt my sister or had anything to do with her disappearance, I'll hunt you down like a dog and make you wish you'd never seen CIRP.''

Adam shot Sarah a frustrated look, then stormed out the door. Sarah ached for him, her own nerves on edge.

As a child, she hadn't understood the inner workings of big business, only that her father and mother were dead, and that her father was a bad man. She was old enough now to know that sometimes people lied. But so many people had told her the same story. The things they'd accused Denise of hit too close to home. Had her father been the traitor they'd said? Could he have been framed by someone else?

Maybe she should talk to Sol about Denise. She touched her cheek, remembering his fury. If she went to him, would they have a repeat scene of the night before?

ANGER RAGED inside Adam. He glanced toward Sarah as they climbed in his car, expecting to see fear and distrust in her eyes, but instead he saw compassion.

For the first time since he'd met her, he realized what it must have been like for her to grow up hearing her father labeled as a traitor. Just the implication that Denise would do something unethical infuriated him. How had Sarah handled the stigma all these years?

He knew Denise wouldn't do anything wrong. And

he would prove it. His gut tightened. Even if it meant implicating Sarah's godfather?

How would she feel if she discovered the only man who'd been a real father to her was corrupt? Would she hate Adam for slandering her godfather?

Probably.

He punched in Clay's number on his cell phone, not bothering to start the car. "Black here. Did anything turn up on Sarah Cutter's wreck yesterday?"

"They found some black paint smudges on the bumper where the other car hit her. We're running a make on it now."

"Anything else?"

"No leads so far."

"What about Gates? Anything new?"

"I talked to his mother again. She still claims he wouldn't harm a fly. That he wouldn't commit suicide."

Adam prayed Gates's mother was right, that Gates hadn't killed Denise.

"Oh, and Sol Santenelli called. Apparently he heard about Sarah Cutter's accident. Santenelli's pretty freaked. Tell Sarah she should call him."

Adam's gaze found the bruise on her cheek, and anger bolted through him. He wasn't sure he'd pass the message along. He didn't want her anywhere near her godfather, not just yet. But did he have the right to keep her from the man who'd raised her?

"He was really worried?" Adam asked past the lump in his throat.

"Sounded like it. Is Sarah with you now?"

"Yeah."

"This getting personal, man?"

Adam wished to hell it wasn't. But he couldn't

deny the ache that built in his body every time he looked at her. "Don't worry, partner. Nothing will interfere with the job."

"Life is more than work, Black."

"Not to me, it's not." Adam clenched his jaw. Life *had* always been about work before. And no matter how much he was starting to care about Sarah Cutter, life would always be about his job.

SARAH LISTENED silently, uncertain as to the direction of Adam's conversation. Had Clay asked about her?

"Mind if we stop by my place so I can pick up a change of clothes?"

She shook her head as he drove away from the research center.

"Clay said your godfather freaked about the accident," Adam said. "Apparently Bernstein talked to him this morning. Santenelli had no idea you'd been in a crash last night."

Had it only been one night? Sarah thought. One night since she'd been terrified, and had lain in Adam's arms, naked and sated from his lovemaking? Feeling closer to him than she'd ever felt to another man before.

"You want to go by and see him?"

She shook her head no. She'd wait until she got home, then maybe send him a message via her phone.

Ten minutes later, they parked in front of a small apartment building in the low-rent side of Savannah. Weeds dotted the sparse grass, a few junky cars filled the parking spaces and the paint on the brown wooden building had peeled in layers. Why did Adam live here? Couldn't he afford a nicer place?

Sarah was curious. She wanted to know more about

him, much more. He acted as if he didn't need anyone, but sometimes she glimpsed a deep loneliness in his eyes that made her want to reach out to him.

"It's not much," Adam said as if he'd read her mind about his apartment. "But all I need's a place to crash at night. And I cut a deal with the landlord. Neighborhoods like this like to have a cop around, helps keep crime down."

Sarah nodded and opened the door, tensing when Adam rushed around to help her. Her ankle was aching, so she let him help her get out, but then pushed him away to hobble by herself, determined that she would stand on her own two feet, literally and figuratively.

Determined that he see her as a strong, independent woman, not an imperfect one.

As soon as they entered his apartment, he pushed aside a stack of laundry on a threadbare sofa and gestured for her to sit, then moved a mismatched footstool over to prop up her ankle. She should have enjoyed his attention, but she hated that he saw her as frail.

"I'll just grab some clothes and pack a duffel."

She grabbed a pad and pencil and wrote, "You don't have to stay with me. I'll be fine with the new security system."

"I'm not leaving you until this is over, Sarah. There's no argument on that one." His dark eyes pinned her. "Besides, I want to talk to Santenelli again. I expect he'll be waiting for you when we get to your place."

She gripped the pencil tightly in her fingers, frowning as he strode to the other room. His absence gave her time to study his apartment. The garage-sale furniture looked ancient, the place devoid of any homey touches. The perfect place for a man who seldom stayed at home.

An oak entertainment unit held a small TV and CD player, with CDs stacked haphazardly on the coffee table. She rummaged through them, curious about his tastes. Billy Joel, Fleetwood Mac, the Stones, a Shawn Mullins one that she herself loved. A guitar sat propped against the side of the unit. Interesting. She didn't know Adam played.

A small bookcase to the side held an assortment of true-crime books. A collection of model cars occupied the second shelf. Had Adam kept them from childhood? Did they hold some sentimental value?

Then a small stack of poetry books, and a songwriting book caught her eye. Did Adam Black, the tough cop who seemed to stand so alone, have a soft spot for poetry? Did he write his own songs? Curious, she picked up the book and thumbed through it, astonished even more when a few loose sheets of paper fell from the book. She couldn't help herself— she unfolded them, her heart squeezing at the scribbled phrases, the crossed-out lines, the beautiful words.

> Silent cries of anguish
> Silent cries of hurt
> Were all wrapped up inside
> In the words that no one heard.

Her fingers tightened around the edges of the pages, the words playing over in her mind. She could almost hear Adam singing them in his husky voice.

Silent cries—could the song possibly be about her?

If he hadn't meant them to be, they certainly fit, she realized. She'd never thought about it, but she had been crying silent tears since she was five.

Not bothering to speak or cry out loud because she'd screamed out for help that horrible night of the explosion, because her screams hadn't mattered. Her parents had died anyway.

A drawer closing in the other room broke through her troubling thoughts. Not wanting to get caught snooping, she quickly stuffed the papers back inside the book and placed it on the shelf. A photograph of Adam's family drew her eye. Adam must have been about fourteen when the picture was taken—even as a teen, he was tall and muscular, yet he had that lean adolescent stature and a look of innocence that was missing today. Denise looked about ten—she was petite with a perky nose and a smile that showed crooked teeth. His father wasn't as tall, and wore a faded shirt and jeans, his mother was slender with the same dark hair and eyes. Her breath caught when she noticed a white cane in his mother's hands—his mother had been blind. Odd, Adam had never mentioned it. Could it be one reason he was drawn to her? Did he feel sorry for her because he understood the problems his mother faced having a handicap?

Disturbed by the thought, she studied the other photo. Denise had been dressed in a cap and gown, holding a doctoral degree. Adam obviously had such a loving family, much more normal than hers, so why would he not want a family of his own as an adult?

Denise's cries rang in her head again. "Help me, please, help me."

Sarah shuddered, and clutched the picture. *We're*

trying to find you, Denise. Just hold on a little while longer.

ADAM WONDERED what Sarah thought about his dingy little apartment, and hated that he cared. Normally he wouldn't give it a second thought. Was she comparing it to the mansion she'd grown up in? To her homey town house with her cat and her cozy fireplace? Would she see him for the low-paid cop he really was? The man who owed so much in loans he'd taken out for Denise's school that he couldn't afford a better place?

He stuffed clothes in a duffel, then shrugged off the matter, telling himself it was better she saw him for himself instead of envisioning some kind of knight in shining armor. Tossing the bag over his shoulder, he strode to the den, surprised to find Sarah holding his guitar on her lap, lightly strumming the strings. She glanced up in embarrassment when she noticed him in the doorway.

Then suddenly she pushed it toward him, silently asking him to play.

"I—I'm not very good," he said, uncomfortable playing for an audience, even an audience of one. Somehow it seemed too intimate, as if he'd be revealing too much about himself. "Besides, we need to get going."

She caught his hand, her lips mouthing the word *please,* and his heart felt an odd pang.

"Please." She handed him a note. "I dreamed of hearing beautiful sounds like laughter and music when I received the implant. So far, I've heard more unpleasant sounds than pleasant ones."

How could he deny her such a heartfelt request?

He parked himself on the sofa beside her, feeling awkward and too damn exposed as he began to strum. She curled her legs up beside her, her floral skirt billowing around bare ankles as she gazed at him. First, he simply tuned the guitar, watching as her eyes drifted shut and her body slowly swayed to the sound. She was so damn beautiful he found himself mesmerized by the way her lips parted, and the subtle smile that lifted the corner of her lips.

Without realizing he was doing it, he began to play Eric Clapton's "Tears in Heaven." The words flowed from him as he sang them in his low baritone, reminding him of the day he had sung the ballad at his parents' funeral. Sarah wiped at moisture in the corner of her eye, but her tender smile voiced her approval. He finished the last verse, a peace washing over him that he hadn't felt in a while. As if she understood the song held a special meaning for him, she picked up one of the model cars from the bookshelf and raised her brow in question.

"My dad and I used to work on them together. It was kind of a hobby."

She smiled, studying the small plastic Corvette.

"He was a mechanic," he found himself telling her. "Dad loved cars, Mom loved Dad. They were poor but they seemed happy."

Her gaze met his, compassion in her eyes once again, but this time he saw something else. Envy that his parents had loved each other? Knowing the things he did about her father now, the past must haunt her.

"They died in a car crash right after my seventeenth birthday." He paused, then continued, unable to stand the silence. "Denise was only thirteen." He put the guitar aside, scrubbing his hands over his face. "I guess if there was anything good about it, at least they died together."

Sarah reached out and covered his hand with hers, heat spearing through him at her touch. She released his hand, wrote another note and handed him the pad again. "So you took care of Denise?"

He nodded, surprised at himself for spilling his life story. "It was tough going at first. Unfortunately Dad wasn't rich, but he had a little money put aside for us to live on. But Denise was so smart. And she'd always dreamed of being a doctor."

"So you put her through school? Did you take out loans?"

He nodded, growing more uncomfortable. But she lifted his hand between hers, then pressed it to her lips and kissed his palm. He gazed into her blue eyes, his body churning with emotions and the desire to take her all over again. To make her his, then and there.

Maybe forever.

The shrill sound of the phone jolted him from the shocking thought. He swallowed, then released her hand, and answered the phone, glad for the interruption.

"Detective Black, this is Robey Burgess. We met before."

Adam froze, one hand on the edge of the table as he listened.

"I've got some information I think you might be interested in."

"What do you want, Burgess?"

"Meet me at the marina tonight."

"Look, if you know something just spit it out."

"I can't, not over the phone." Burgess lowered his voice. "I have something to show you. Something that will tell you where you can find your sister."

Chapter Eighteen

"What do we do now?" Sarah wrote.

"I guess we find out what information he has. Or what he thinks he has."

Sarah checked her watch. They had several hours until midnight. "Let's go talk to Sol."

"Are you sure?"

"I know you have questions about the center and Dr. Bradford didn't answer them. Maybe Sol will."

Adam lowered himself down beside her on the sofa, and touched her cheek with his finger. "Sarah, I realize you love him even though he hurt you last night."

Sarah squeezed his hand, then wrote. "I do love him, and I don't think he would hurt your sister, Adam. You don't know him like I do. He took me in and raised me like a daughter."

"I understand that."

"We have to find Denise, and if Sol knows something, then we need to talk to him."

"Okay, but I'll get him to meet us at your place. I want to talk to him on neutral turf."

Sarah nodded, and listened silently as Adam called her godfather. He was supposedly out, so Adam left a message for him to meet them at Sarah's, then phoned Denise's ex-husband as they drove off in Adam's car. Earlier, he'd asked Russell to find out if the German company visiting the center was looking at Denise's research or if any other companies or scientists might be interested. Hopefully, being on the inside would enable Russell to get the information Adam couldn't. Clay was supposed to be checking any competitors that might exist. He'd also asked him to have someone pull up all the information on Sarah's father they could find. "Any news on that research company?"

"Lips are sealed tighter around here than a nuclear plant," Russell said. "Have you learned anything else about that psycho Gates?"

"'Fraid not. If he didn't abduct Denise and someone at the center did, do you have any idea where they might have taken her? Some hidden labs?"

"Maybe. I've never been to the facility on Nighthawk Island. That takes special clearance." Russell sighed. "And I know there's a couple of buildings they're renovating on Whistlestop but they're not open yet."

"They could be hiding her in any of those places," Adam said.

"I do know this. Sol Santenelli oversees everything that goes on at the center. The other founder, Hughes, is the silent partner, but Santenelli is a control freak. Has his eye on every company that joins the research park."

Adam stole a glance at Sarah, his chest tightening. Seconds later, they arrived at Sarah's and found Sol Santenelli waiting on the doorstep. Adam told Russell to keep searching, and hung up, although Adam still wasn't convinced he could trust the man. What if he had led him astray by planting suspicions about the research company? Then again, why go to the trouble with Gates already under scrutiny?

Unless Russell knew Gates hadn't killed Denise. The only way he could know that was if he knew her kidnapper or if he had killed her himself.

SARAH SHIVERED at the look of fury on her godfather's face when he saw Adam help her out of the car.

"Sarah, darling, are you all right?" Fury turned to concern when Sol swept her into his arms. "I've been out of my mind with worry over you."

Sarah stiffened in his embrace, confused even more by the true anguish in his eyes. Still, she couldn't shake the fear and hurt she'd felt when he'd slapped her.

"God, honey, when they called and said my Honda had been involved in an accident—"

"It wasn't an accident," Adam said sharply.

Sol's legs buckled slightly, and he leaned on his cane. "What do you mean?"

"Someone intentionally hit Sarah and ran her off the embankment. A few more seconds and she might not have crawled out of the car alive."

"Good God, do you know who did it? Was it the same person who broke into her place?"

"We don't know yet," Adam said curtly.

Sol swiped perspiration off his face. "Sarah, when I realized you'd left and taken the Honda, I went crazy. I've been calling and calling you. I was so afraid you were hurt, and that you were so angry you wouldn't see me again."

"I'm fine, Sol," Sarah signed, unable to stay angry when Sol looked so utterly tortured.

He pressed a kiss to her cheek, touching the spot where he had hit her, his bottom lip quivering.

"I have to ask you some questions," Adam said.

"I don't understand," Sol snapped. "Why aren't you trying to find this maniac who tried to kill my goddaughter?"

"I am," Adam said. "I think the threats on her life have to do with my sister's disappearance."

Sarah dropped her hands from Sol's and signed, "Let's go inside. I'll make some coffee and we can talk."

Her godfather didn't look pleased, but he followed them inside. A few minutes later, they sat in the den with coffee.

"Tell me about this German company coming in to town." Adam braced his elbows on his knees leaning forward in an intimidating move. "I want to know what they're here to buy, how their visit relates to my sister's work and what the hell you've done with her."

ADAM STEELED HIMSELF when Sarah flinched. She obviously hadn't planned on his accusing her godfather of being directly involved in Denise's abduction, but if Santenelli had the power Adam thought he did, he most likely had dirty hands.

"The company's interest is confidential. The Germans aren't interested in your sister's research. In fact, I didn't even know the details of your sister's work until we met and you raised suspicions about her. Then I started checking around." Santenelli paused, sipping his coffee calmly.

Adam ground his teeth. "Listen, Santenelli, I have reason to believe Jerome Simms was murdered because of an announcement he was about to make regarding his work. One week after his death, your company sold a product for a hefty amount. My guess is that it was Simms's work."

"You're guessing, Detective Black. You have no proof because there is none. And the papers said that research assistant killed your sister because he was infatuated with her."

"The evidence is inconclusive." Adam prayed he hadn't gone off on a tangent here, that he was looking for something that didn't exist because he wanted to believe Denise was still alive.

Santenelli began to pace, ranting about the wonderful research the center sponsored. "Do you know we're close to finding a cure for AIDS, and we have a compound ready for trial studies which might wipe out breast cancer completely?" He wiped at a bead of sweat on his forehead. "We're in the business of furthering science, not killing our scientists to steal their work! What good would that do us?" Sol turned to Sarah, his expression pleading. "Tell him, Sarah. You've seen how hard I've worked to get this center off the ground, you know how dedicated I am to medical science, how closely we've screened the companies and scientists who come to work here."

"Yeah, my sister was thrilled when she was hired on," Adam said in a low voice, "I just wonder if her dedication got her killed."

SARAH WAS GRATEFUL when Adam finally excused himself to phone Clay. The tension between her godfather and Adam had been almost unbearable.

Besides, she wanted to talk to Sol alone. She had to get up the nerve to ask about her father again.

But Sol interrupted her before she had a chance. "Sarah, honey, what's going on with you and this detective?"

"Nothing," Sarah signed. "I'm simply trying to help him find his sister, and he's trying to protect me."

"Is that all he's doing?" Fatherly concern tinged Sol's voice. Sarah had always relied on visual clues to determine underlying meanings. She'd never realized how much the inflection of a person's voice could suggest their feelings.

She nodded. Business was all Adam would let there be.

"I saw the way he was looking at you, Sarah. Like a *man,* not like a police officer."

Sarah couldn't fight a small smile. "He is a man, Sol. But don't worry. I can take care of myself."

Sol rubbed a freckled hand over his eyes, looking tired. "I don't know. I'm worried about you. And if you think there's a future with this cop, you're wrong. You deserve better, honey. Do you know what kind of salary they make?"

"I don't care about money," Sarah signed.

"So, you are involved?"

"No."

"Good. Just look what's happened already. Being tied up with this man has almost gotten you killed."

"It's not his fault his sister is missing."

"It's not yours, either," Sol said, his voice harsh. "And you don't owe this man anything."

"You're wrong, Sol," Sarah signed. "I owe him my life. You're forgetting about the man who attacked me right here in my apartment.'' She took a deep breath for courage. ''Dr. Bradford implied that Adam's sister might have run off with the research to sell it herself.''

Sol's gray eyes flickered with interest. ''That's always a possibility.''

''Adam is convinced it's not true, and I don't think so, either,'' Sarah signed. ''But it made me wonder about Dad. Is there any way the charges that were brought against him were false?''

Weariness pulled at the age lines on her godfather's face. ''Honey, I want to tell you that it's possible, but—'' Sol's voice cracked ''—the investigators found very convincing evidence.''

Sarah wound her fingers together in her lap, fighting disappointment.

''Now, try to forget about all that. It happened years ago. Focus on your future.''

''I can't do that until we find Adam's sister,'' Sarah signed.

Sol's face blanched while Denise's frightened voice replayed itself in Sarah's mind. She pressed her hands over her ears, the low sound of voices crackling in and out. Was it Denise? She'd never forget that cry, or the anguish in Adam's eyes when he'd sung ''Tears in Heaven'' earlier. She sensed his grief and worry, had felt it as if it were a tangible part of herself. He'd sang it at his parents' funeral. She prayed he didn't have to sing it at his sister's as well.

ADAM STOOD in the alcove of the kitchen dialing Clay's number, his jaw clenching at the direction of Sol Santenelli's conversation. Santenelli was right— he couldn't give Sarah the kind of life she deserved.

His job was dangerous, his salary paltry and his romance skills nonexistent.

Then why did it bother him so much that she hadn't argued with Santenelli about him? From the one-sided conversation, it sounded as if she'd denied a personal involvement.

That was what he wanted, wasn't it?

Clay answered the line. "Black, I've been trying to reach you."

"What do you have?"

"Found out some interesting info on Russell Harley. It seems he got into some financial trouble a while back, overextended himself when he bought that house and boat."

"So?"

"So, Denise had a big life-insurance policy. Guess who she named as the benefactor?"

"Russell." Adam cursed. "Dammit, Clay, she never took his name off the policy?"

"Afraid not. She was probably so busy working she never even gave it a thought."

"So, how much was it worth?"

"A million."

Adam rubbed the front of his head where a headache started to pulse. First Gates, then the center, now Russell—he didn't know which way to turn. He felt as if he were spinning his wheels in quicksand.

"So that would provide him with motivation?"

"And he had security clearance so he could go anywhere on the facility he wanted."

"He also had access to Denise's files. Hell, he might be the very one selling her research to the Germans."

Clay hesitated. "Could be. Tell me about his boat."

"He called it the *Windjammer*. It's at the Grist Mill Marina."

The same marina where he was meeting Burgess tonight, Adam thought. Another coincidence?

"Did you check it out?"

"I'm getting a search warrant now."

"Good." Adam explained about the reporter's call and asked Clay to meet him at midnight for backup.

"On the other hand," Clay added, "one of the lab techs at the center said Gates was agitated the last couple of weeks. According to her, Gates liked Denise, but he was worried she might be getting back with her husband."

"Shit." Adam slammed a fist on the bed.

"She also said Russell refused to sign the final divorce papers, that he was holding out, hoping for a reconciliation."

Or wanting to make sure the insurance claim was legal. Dammit, he should have seen this coming.

"Thinking Denise might go back to her husband might have been enough to set Gates off," Clay speculated. "The old if I can't have you no one else will mentality."

"And if it failed, he might have gone off the deep end and killed himself."

And her, too.

Gates or Russell—both had motive and opportunity.

Adam just prayed Burgess knew the answer. And that she was still alive when they found her.

SARAH STARED at the boats docked at the near-deserted marina, praying they would find Denise. And when Adam found her, she wanted to be there to meet her.

Or to comfort Adam if he found her body instead.

Adam parked in front of the Grist Mill Saloon at the marina, cutting off the engine so that the sound sputtered in the quiet of the night. Water lapped at the edges of the dock, the whisper of an evening breeze stirred the leaves and the smells of salt water and fish wafted around her, seemingly calm.

But Adam's labored breath cut to the bone.

The past three hours had dragged by, each moment filled with escalating tension. Adam obviously didn't believe her godfather and suspected Sol knew more than he was telling. Then again, he'd relayed the information his partner had given him about Russell and Donny Gates, so he was keeping an open mind.

Suspecting everyone.

The clock read 11:55.

Five more minutes until they met Robey Burgess.

"He said to meet him at the slip where the *Bluebird* was docked. Wait here."

Sarah grabbed his hand, indicating she wanted to go with him.

Adam nodded as he scanned the area. Only two boats had lights on, the others appeared vacant. It was too early for summer vacation and spring break. They crossed the sidewalk silently, bore to the right and walked onto the wooden dock. The planks sounded hollow beneath their feet, the water slapping the bank below them. Sarah held Adam's hand, still favoring her right foot. Stars shimmered along the edge of the water, and the occasional sound of a fish splashing broke the silence.

Down past three sport cruisers and a houseboat the *Bluebird* sat on the right. It was a thirty-six-foot speedboat.

Sarah frowned at the strong odor of sea, and something else…garbage maybe?

Adam threw his hand back to stop her, and Sarah gasped.

A man's body floated in the water, one foot caught on the anchor of the boat, blood swirling around him.

Suddenly the sound of a gunshot split the air, and Adam dove, knocking her down to the hard wooden dock beneath them.

Chapter Nineteen

Adam rolled to the edge of the dock onto the boat, covering Sarah's body with his, then yanked his gun from his holster and looked around. Where the hell had the shots come from? One of the other boats? Down the dock? And where was Clay?

It was so damn dark he couldn't see anything but the shadows flittering along the bank and the row of boats. The boat rocked with the lull of the water, echoing in the silence, but he couldn't distinguish any other sounds, except Sarah's quick breathing. Finally, he gave himself a second to check her. "Are you okay?"

Her blue eyes stared at him, wide and frightened, but she nodded. Relief surged through him.

He rose slightly on his knees to search for the shooter, but another shot pinged through the air and he ducked, plastering his body to Sarah's again to shield her. Seconds later, footsteps pounded in the distance, and a small dark car geared up and screeched from the parking lot. He jumped up and ran down the dock, but the car disappeared in the dust. Afraid to leave Sarah alone, he grabbed his cell phone to call for backup, then jogged back down the dock to her.

She was sitting with her knees up, backed into the corner of the front of the boat, her eyes wide as she stared at the dead man's body floating in the water. Adam wanted to comfort her, but seconds later, Clay appeared. Minutes later, a team of investigators had arrived.

Robey Burgess's name would make the paper the next morning, Adam thought, only this time his name would be in the headlines instead of a byline. And Adam might not ever find out what Burgess had known about his sister.

SARAH WATCHED in horror as the crime scene investigators taped off the area. She hadn't liked the sleazy reporter, but she hadn't wanted him dead. And to see his bloody body floating in the inlet brought the threat to her own life too close to home.

Other cops searched for the killer on the surrounding boats, while Adam oversaw police go through Burgess's pockets after they'd finally lifted him from the water. She knew he hoped to find some notebook or name that Burgess had planned to pass on to Adam, and she felt his frustration when he came up empty.

"We can't be certain that Burgess was killed because he was meeting you," an officer named Turner argued. "He wrote for the tabloids. He probably ticked off a lot of people over the years."

Adam cursed. "I know what I know. Burgess's death only confirms that whoever has my sister is worried we're going to find her and figure out their plan."

"What about Gates?"

"I'm not convinced Gates killed her," Adam said gruffly. "Burgess was meeting me with information about Denise, so someone must have killed Burgess to silence him."

"But Turner has a point," Clay conceded. "Burgess had a lot of enemies. And you've been stirring up bad publicity for that research center. You might have ticked off someone, so we could be talking about two different things here, maybe two different motives and unrelated crimes."

Adam obviously wasn't buying it, but Sarah wondered if there might be truth in the policeman's speculations. If this German company was on the verge of making the deal with CIRP and someone at the center was worried she or Adam would ruin the deal, it might be reason to kill them.

Sol had been upset when she'd asked questions about her father....

Adam turned to Clay. "I'm not ruling out any possibilities now. But I intend to search Burgess's home and office right away. Surely he left backup files on the stories he's been working on."

"Will do."

"There's one more place here I have to check."

Clay cocked his head to the side. "Russell's boat?"

"Yeah. I'm going to the *Windjammer* now, then to Burgess's place."

Sarah stood. Wherever Adam went, she was going, too.

ADAM DIDN'T WANT to believe that his own brother-in-law might be responsible for his sister's disappearance and that he had been misleading them, but he'd been a cop too damn long not to follow every lead. In murder cases, statistics proved the spouse was to blame.

He prayed this time statistics were wrong.

Sarah touched his arm lightly, and he read the questions in her eyes, so he explained about Denise's insurance policy.

Horror darkened her eyes, then a quiet understanding passed between them so subtly that Adam felt his chest constrict. He'd never shared that kind of silent communication with anyone before. It was almost as if she felt his pain, as if the two of them together made one.

"I have to check out his boat," he said, ignoring the disturbing thought of being tied to Sarah forever. Hadn't he learned from Pamela's death that getting sidetracked cost lives? He never wanted that to happen to Sarah.

The *Windjammer* sat in the last slip to the right, a sixty-foot yacht that must have cost his brother-in-law a small fortune. Adam paused on the dock, his heartbeat accelerating.

The boat had been boarded up for the winter or at least in preparation for bad weather.

Or since Russell had stashed a body onboard?

But if he'd killed Denise, he most likely wouldn't have kept her body—he would have dumped it into the ocean. A shudder gripped him.

He'd check with the security guard to see when Russell had last been up to the boat. But now, he had to get inside. He removed the protective tarp from the cockpit, and moved onto the deck.

His pulse clamored as he finally opened the door and peered inside. Darkness hung in the interior and a musty stale scent permeated the air as if the boat hadn't been used for a long time. Careful to keep Sarah behind him, Adam turned on his flashlight and scanned the cabin. Empty. He searched both the master stateroom and the two side berths.

"No sign of anything." Adam exhaled, not knowing whether to be relieved or more worried. "I know it's late and you've got to be exhausted, Sarah. Do you want me to take you to a hotel somewhere while I go to Burgess's?"

Sarah shook her head, gesturing that she wanted to go with him.

Adam stroked her cheek, his fingers tracing along her soft skin as if the touch could somehow take away his pain. He had to keep going, he had to keep believing he would find his sister. "Then let's go to Robey Burgess's place and see what we find there. I want to search it before the killer does."

SARAH SHIVERED with exhaustion as they entered the reporter's small, dingy apartment. Dust covered the outdated furniture in the one-room efficiency, and cigarette burns and stains dotted the rust-colored carpet. Adam switched on a lamp on the scarred end table.

"Burgess obviously wasn't a neatnick." Adam indicated the mountain of laundry piled on the sofa and the newspapers scattered on the floor.

Or a health nut, either, Sarah surmised, noting the pizza boxes and fast-food wrappers overflowing the trash in the corner of the dingy kitchen nook.

"I'm going to search his desk. If you want, you can rest on the sofa."

Sarah frowned, wishing she could help, but not

knowing what to do. She sank into the faded plaid recliner and closed her eyes. Her foot ached and her ears were ringing from the gunshots fired at them earlier. Images and sounds bombarded her—the sight of the man's dead body floating in the water, the sharp ping of the bullets, the low sound of Denise's voice crying out in the night....

ADAM YANKED OPEN the drawers of Burgess's desk, not surprised to find a jumble of office supplies, sticky notes and files that seemed to have no order. Frustrated, he sat down and began to sort through them, tossing outdated files and clippings from the tabloids. Finally, he came across one marked CIRP. Inside, he found articles dating back to the beginning of the center's opening, photographs of all the companies and the dates they'd been brought into the research center, articles on Simms's death, a faded yellow clipping about Sarah's father. He read the article, shuddering when he thought of all Sarah had to cope with in her young life. Yet Sarah had fought not to be dependent.

He stared at a photo of the explosion. A storm raged around them as Santenelli carried Sarah to safety amidst the blaze. The horror and fear on the man's face was obvious as he clutched the five-year-old child in his arms. Adam's lungs hurt as he let out a breath. She'd been so tiny, so damn young.

Another article fell from the pile and he skimmed it, his eyes narrowing at the title. ''Charles Cutter Thought To Be Alive. Ex-navy lieutenant and renowned scientist, Charles Cutter is thought to have absconded with cutting-edge technology after killing his wife and faking his own death. FBI agent Trevor

Donovan believes Cutter sold the technology to the Russians and is now in hiding.''

Adam scrubbed a hand over his face. Had Sarah seen the article?

Obviously, Burgess suspected something might be going on at the center or he wouldn't have all this information. He booted up Burgess's computer and searched through the file manager, his chest tight. If Sarah's father was alive and had been hiding all these years, could he be responsible for all this trouble? How would she feel to learn he was alive, that he'd deserted her? Could Santenelli know where her father was hiding? Had he been protecting her from her father all these years? Or had he been protecting Charles Cutter?

The ramifications complicated everything.

He had to find out what else Burgess had discovered, if he'd already been working on a slant to his story. A few minutes later, he'd scanned the computer, but he found nothing on the research center.

Not one single file.

Odd. Maybe Burgess had kept the information on a disk for safety. He stood and rummaged through the drawers. Nothing. Frustrated, he searched the apartment, frantically clawing through his closet, but still came up empty.

Behind him, a squeaking sound broke through the silence. He glanced at the door. Someone was trying to open it.

SARAH HAD FALLEN into a restless sleep. But she jerked awake when Adam grabbed her and pulled her to the floor. He pushed her head down with his hand, forcing her to crouch behind the sofa, sending panic skittering up her spine.

Someone was turning the doorknob, opening the door.

Adam pulled his gun. Sarah's heart stopped when a tall man stepped inside.

Chapter Twenty

The overhead light flickered on and a woman followed the man. "I heard someone in here," the woman said in a high-pitched voice.

Bright light flickered off the metal of a security guard's gun. He had to be at least sixty, Sarah thought. The woman who stood beside him wore her gray hair in a bun, wielding her cane out for protection.

Adam stood slowly but kept his hand on Sarah's back, holding her down. "Relax, folks, Savannah Police Department." Adam's badge flickered in the light and the woman gasped.

"What are you doing in here?" the guard asked, his deep voice trying for bravado but failing.

"I'm here on an official investigation. Sir, please put your weapon away."

The guard's hand shook as he dropped the weapon to his side. Adam stuffed his gun in his holster, and pulled Sarah up beside him.

"Oh, my." The woman's hand fluttered to her chest.

"It's okay, ma'am," Adam said in a quiet voice. "Are you the owner of the apartments?"

"Yes."

"I didn't mean to frighten you, ma'am. I would have asked you to let me in, but it was so late I didn't want to disturb you."

"Mind telling us what this is all about?" The man recovered enough to steady his voice.

"I'm afraid your tenant, Mr. Burgess, was killed tonight. I'm looking for clues as to who might have murdered him."

The old lady swayed and the guard caught her. Adam helped her to a chair. Sarah hurried to retrieve her a glass of water. A few minutes later, when they were fairly certain they didn't have to call 911, and they'd learned that the woman's name was Elsie Clemmens and the guard's, Herman Porter, Adam continued.

"I think Mr. Burgess might have been killed because of a story he was working on, so I need to go through his files."

"Oh, dear." Elsie fluttered her hand again. "He was afraid something might happen to him."

"What do you mean?" Adam asked.

Elsie's age-spotted hand tapped at her chin. "The other day he came to me and—and he seemed distracted." She stood, wobbling on thin knobby legs. "He gave me a package to hold."

"What kind of package?"

"I don't know what was in it," Elsie said, looking agitated. "But he said if anything ever happened to him, I should give it to the police."

"Can you get it for me now?"

The old lady nodded, and allowed Herman to help her to the door. It seemed like forever to Sarah before they returned. When they did, Adam tore open the plain manila envelope.

"Computer disks," he said calmly. "These must be the files I've been looking for."

Sarah prayed they told them where to find Denise.

IT WAS NEARLY midnight when they made it to Sarah's, but Adam's heart raced as he opened the files. Sarah read over his shoulder as he scanned the notes Burgess had made regarding the research center, articles about the center, photographs of the buildings and several scientists. Articles about the explosion that had killed Sarah's parents, a description of the thunderstorm that had rocked the area that same night, flooding areas. Interviews with the psychologist who had treated Sarah after the explosion describing what she had seen that night through crude childhood drawings.

An article about Sarah's father possibly being alive followed.

Sarah paled beside him.

He could see the worry, the uncertainty in her eyes.

Her family, what little she had left, might be destroyed when he got his sister back.

And he had no way of promising her that it might not happen.

"Did you know about this?"

She nodded.

"Why didn't you tell me?"

She simply shrugged, a wariness in her expression that told him a lot. She didn't trust him. Hurt and anger slammed into him.

"Is it true? Is your father alive?" He rammed his hand through his hair. "Could he be responsible for all this havoc? Could he be a part of the German company?''

Sarah shook her head in denial, then wrote. ''I don't know. That's what I asked Sol about the night he hit me, but he said police found evidence my dad did die in that fire.''

''Have you received any gifts, notes, anything over the years to indicate he might be alive and in hiding?''

''No. Nothing.''

''You could have told me, Sarah.''

She clenched her hands in her lap but said nothing. He turned back to the files, disappointed although he didn't know why. If he were in her shoes, would he have told?

Seconds later, his pulse jumped when he stumbled across a set of maps—maps which detailed the research facilities, the buildings on Catcall, plans for the ones on Whistlestop and a drawing of two cites on Nighthawk Island. Stars highlighted one of the buildings.

''My father's office was in that building,'' Sarah wrote. ''But Sol told me the entire place had been destroyed.''

According to the plans, though, the buildings had been renovated and were being used for highly classified government projects. Her godfather had lied about the building.

Had he lied about other things, as well?

HAD SOL LIED about other things? Sarah wondered as they knocked on Russell Harley's door thirty minutes later. Like whether or not her father was alive.

If he was, could he have somehow come back?

Maybe joined the center? Could he be hiding out on Nighthawk Island working in secret for the center? Could he be behind all this trouble? Maybe working for the Germans?

The possibility was far-fetched. Still, Sarah couldn't stifle the uncertainty, the very reason she wouldn't let Adam talk her into not going with him. If they discovered something about her father, she wanted to be there.

Adam pounded on Russell's door.

Russell opened the door, tugging on a robe, his eyes widening when he saw Adam. "Do you have news about Denise? Did you find her?"

His hair was sticking straight out, his wire-rimmed glasses sitting crookedly on his nose and he had dark circles beneath his eyes as if he hadn't been sleeping well. Sarah realized Adam still didn't quite trust the man, but from the genuine worry in Russell's eyes, it was obvious he still loved Denise.

"No, but I think I may know where she is."

Russell ushered them in. "Where?"

"In one of those buildings on Nighthawk Island. I want you to help me get there."

Sarah expected Russell to argue, but instead he agreed. "Let me change. It won't be easy, but we'll take my boat."

Adam nodded. A few seconds later, he emerged.

"Tell me about the insurance policy, Russell," Adam said as they climbed in Adam's car. "You get a million if Denise turns up dead?"

Russell frowned. "Dammit, Black, I don't care about the money."

"But you're in debt and I know you refused to sign divorce papers."

''Half of America is in debt! And I didn't sign those divorce papers because I was hoping for a reconciliation.''

Sarah twisted her hands in her lap as they drove toward the marina, wincing when Adam explained about breaking into Russell's boat earlier and searching it.

''You really care about Denise, Harley?'' Adam checked the backpack he'd thrown together with emergency supplies, studying Russell as they pulled into the marina.

''Absolutely. I want Denise back.'' Russell's voice wavered. ''That is, if Denise is willing to compromise. I really love her, Adam, but I do want a family.''

An odd look settled in Adam's eyes, a yearning that made Sarah's stomach twist. Would he ever consider a family of his own? A little boy with thick dark hair and dark eyes…

Probably not, she thought, her heart aching. Not after she'd kept secrets from him. Especially if her own family had played a part in hurting his sister.

DARK CLOUDS hovered above them, moving in from the west, the first sign of the thunderstorm brewing in the sky. Even without it, though, a heavy mist shrouded Nighthawk Island giving it a dark, eerie feeling. Adam wrapped a blanket about Sarah, shielding her from the growing winds with his body as Russell motored the boat into the cove. She'd been shivering the entire ride, her face pale with worry.

''This spot can't be seen from the security tower,'' Russell explained, his voice losing its resonance in the wind. ''If you follow that trail through the sea oats, you'll come out at Building A. If someone has Denise, that's where they'd take her. The two buildings on the other side are highly restricted because of decontamination requirements.'' Russell began tying the boat up just as the first few raindrops splattered onto the shell. ''It'll be tough to get in from there. I'll go with you.''

''No, stay here and be ready to get us out of here if we find her. The fewer of us crossing the island, the less chance we have of being noticed. But we may have to stop and rest.'' Adam indicated Russell's cell phone and radio. ''I've got my cell phone. If I call or if we're not back by noon, get my partner over here with backup immediately.''

Russell nodded and climbed off the deck.

Adam studied him for a long moment, trying to decide whether to trust him or not. Finally he decided he had no choice. He took Sarah's hand and led her across the island.

A FEW MINUTES LATER, they raced along the edge of the shore, veering off through the thick sea oats. Thunder crackled and popped, waves thrashed against the rocks, the sounds slamming into Sarah. Wind hurled sand into their faces while lightning zigzagged across the dark sky, shooting a fiery blaze that sent shivers up Sarah's spine.

Adam shielded her with his body as best he could, pulling her along, and steadying her when she stumbled in the wet sand. They ran through the brush close to a mile, crunching shells and other sea debris beneath their feet, the storm escalating in its intensity.

Another loud clap of thunder rent the air and Sarah froze, memories of that haunting night of the explosion descending over her like a wave engulfing her into the tide.

Adam paused, lightning streaking his face with shades of gold, illuminating the worry in his eyes. ''Sarah, come on, we'll find shelter.''

She could barely hear his voice above the horrendous howl of the wind. He curved his arm around her waist and guided her along, using one hand to push aside the thick brush. She slipped on a piece of tree bark and clutched his arm, her nails digging into his damp shirt. Her hair was soaked, the long strands matted against her cheeks, but she pushed on, determined to fight the ghosts that haunted her with every stormy night.

Still, her mother's face flashed in front of her, as if she were standing on the cliff, flames shooting around her, tearing her from Sarah's arms. Sarah froze again, the horror of the image achingly real.

Adam pulled her into his embrace, and suddenly led them into a cave created by the rocks of the cliff. Inside, the storm echoed off the jagged rock walls and Sarah curved her hands over her ears, sank to her knees, then rocked herself back and forth, trying to drown them out.

Voices echoed in her head, bombarding her. Denise's crying haunted her like a low careening wail. She pressed her hands over the sound, hating the anguish she could hear in the other woman's voice.

Lightning struck a tree in the distance, and suddenly she was five years old, lying on the sofa taking a nap. A loud clap of thunder burst into the room, waking her.

''Run, Sarah run!''

Sarah dashed toward her mother, but stumbled and

fell. Her mother appeared in the doorway. "Get out, Sarah. Run!"

But another explosion hit and wood splintered and rained down around her. The floor erupted into flames, they were eating at her mother, shooting up the walls....

ADAM HAD SEEN the photos in the articles Burgess had. It had been storming the night Sarah's parents were killed, the night she'd lost her hearing.

She was reliving it now.

His heart clenched, Sarah's pain becoming his own as he saw the agony in her face. What must it have been like to witness your mother burn to death? Especially at the hands of your father?

He had to get through to her somehow, to bring her out of the misery. He removed a fleece blanket from the backpack and spread it on the ground, then knelt and pulled Sarah into his arms, urging her to lie back in the corner of the cave where it was warm and dry. She was shivering, her teeth chattering, tears streaming down her already wet face. He brushed her hair back and tilted her chin so she had to look at him, but her eyes were glazed and filled with anguish.

"Sarah, honey, it's Adam, you're here with me, now—you're safe." He soothed her with comforting words, rocking her in his arms, hating the helplessness he felt.

Knowing he needed to warm her, he began to undress her, slowly peeling away the silky fabric of the blouse, then her jeans. She relented, searching his face, silently pleading for him to make her pain go away.

He stripped off his own clothes, telling himself he

would only warm her. He wouldn't take her now, not again. So he wrapped his body around her, letting his strength soak up the sorrow and shock.

"It was storming the night of the explosion, wasn't it?" he whispered.

She nodded against his chest, clinging to him as he rubbed his hands up and down her arms.

"You woke to the sound of thunder? Then the house caught fire?"

She nodded again, a low whimper erupting.

He soothed her and stroked her back, pressing gentle kisses along her brow where a tiny scar marred her hairline. He was frustrated not being able to fully communicate with her—it must be frustrating for her all the time. "And you saw your father, didn't you? You thought he was going to save you and your mother?"

Slowly, she lifted her gaze to his, tears slipping down her cheeks as she looked into his eyes, the truth so painful he felt her agony deep inside.

No wonder she hadn't spoken since that horrible night—she'd probably cried out for her father. But he'd only stood by to watch them die. Like the nighthawk that preyed on the weak.

Unable to control the rage that rose inside him, his own eyes grew moist, and a lump formed in his throat. His father hadn't been much financially, but he had loved him and Denise. And that love had meant more than any money he might have given them.

Dear God, he'd been a fool to worry about the material things Santenelli had given her. She would have gladly traded them for her father's love any day.

He didn't want to hurt her more if he discovered

her godfather and the center were involved with Denise's disappearance.

Her ragged breath tore out in gulps. So he began to sing one of his favorite songs, an old hit from Don Henley, "The Heart of the Matter."

Finally, she seemed to calm, the tremors in her body subsiding, her breathing steadying to a low whisper. She was exhausted and they both needed sleep before they could go any further. Her fine-boned hands reached up and tentatively touched his chest, her fingers tangling in the thick dark hair, her breath brushing his neck. He pressed soft gentle kisses along her hair, her forehead, her nose, her cheeks, whispering that he would keep her safe, that everything would be all right.

He only wished he believed it.

Chapter Twenty-One

Sarah was falling in love with Adam.

She soaked up his warmth and the comfort of his embrace, the horror of the storm and her memories abating as Adam's strength melted into her. His skin felt hot, the coarse hair on his chest sending a dozen sensations skittering up her spine.

Everything that had happened to bring them together, the danger, the emotions, the hot lust spiraling between them surged to renewed heights as his gaze found hers. His pupils were dilated, his jaw clenched tight, the hunger in his expression fierce—and all for her.

Nothing else mattered at that moment. Not the storm or the unanswered questions about her father, not even the fact that he would walk away from her soon.

She wanted him to kiss her. To touch her and make her forget the bad memories, to make her come alive with memories of him, memories she could take with her forever.

Her hand brushed his chest, rubbing over his nipple, and she smiled when his body stiffened with arousal. The thick hair on his leg brushed against her thigh as he moved his leg over her, tangling his leg with hers. She stroked his calf with her foot, rubbing slowly up and down the bulging muscle, and cuddled closer to him so her belly brushed his sex. He was hard and big and so damn sexy.

"Sarah—"

She pressed her finger to his lips, begging him with her eyes to make love to her. Afraid he might pull away, and aching to give herself to him with an abandon she'd never felt before, she kissed his chest, nuzzling her face in his warmth, dipping one hand lower to tease his sex, then stroke his swollen flesh. His masculine scent engulfed her.

He watched her with an intensity that stole her breath, then a low growl erupted from deep in his throat. She smiled again, this time biting his nipple, then suckling it gently. His breath caught, and he tilted her chin up, forcing her to stare into his soulful eyes. Hunger, concern, passion, tightened the air between them.

"I want you like I've never wanted a woman, Sarah," he murmured huskily. "But I don't want to hurt you."

"You won't," she mouthed softly, grateful the voices in her head had finally gone silent. She lifted her hand and slowly signed, "I want you, Adam."

Even without words, he understood her message. His eyes lit with a smile so full of tenderness and desire that her throat closed. Lightning zigzagged through the opening of the cave, illuminating the rugged plains of his face, the thunder mimicking the rapid pounding of her heart as his hands swept over her breasts. His breath fanned her cheek as he lowered his head and captured her mouth with his.

Tongues mated, bodies moved in synchronized rhythm, passion exploded between them. His hands kneaded her breasts, torturing her nipples while his tongue danced inside her mouth. He laved her neck with his kisses, then her breasts, suckling each one so that the loud sound echoed in the dark cavern. Heat pooled inside her, a delicious warmth of sensations building inside her body, charging every pore with hunger and love. She'd never imagined wanting a man so much, being able to release her inhibitions to share the erotic joining of their bodies, yet with Adam, she couldn't imagine not being with him this way.

She clawed at his back as he lowered his head, trailing kisses along her abdomen, pulling down her lacy panties with his hands, then moved lower to the insides of her thighs. His long black hair brushed her stomach, then he parted her legs with his hands and placed his mouth to her, suckling greedily.

Sarah thought she might explode. She wanted him inside her. He gave her the sweet, erotic gift of his tongue instead.

Moaning silently, she pulled at his hands, but he deepened the torture by thrusting his tongue inside her. Her breath hitched, the ache building. With a growl of pure animal lust, he rolled her over and stretched his body on top of her, bracing his arms on the ground beside hers as he stroked her legs with his own hair-dusted ones, the course texture creating sensual friction against her smooth skin. His sex pulsed against her backside and she moaned, parting her legs, not caring how she looked as she silently begged him to take her.

He denied her still.

Instead he brushed her hair aside with one hand, and nibbled at her neck, kissing the sensitive skin below her ears. Murmuring erotic words in her hair, he pushed a finger inside her, stroking, torturing her more. With a satisfied sigh, he removed it, then slid two fingers inside her, deeper, deeper, stretching her with each thrust.

Rumbling a husky, erotic endearment, he dropped kisses along her back, lower, lower until she wanted to cry out for him to stop, to plunge his shaft inside her.

"I want you so bad I can't stand it," he growled.

Sarah whimpered, hating the desperation she felt, knowing Adam could do whatever he wanted with her now and she was helpless to deny him.

Then he crawled above her, pressed his sex at the tip of her buttocks and stroked downward. He pressed her hands on the blanket so she couldn't move, then spread her legs apart with his knee, and finally with one hard thrust, rammed his sex inside her. Sarah whimpered and bucked upward, the tightness, the pressure of his body inside hers almost unbearable. He took her fast and hard, pumping inside her with such hot abandon that the tidal wave of need she'd felt building exploded inside her. Tremors of passion shook her as he rammed into her again and again, then a gut-wrenching moan of pleasure tore from him and he took her to heaven.

ADAM COULDN'T EXPLAIN what had overcome him, but when he'd looked into Sarah's sultry eyes and seen how much she'd wanted him, the fierce need to possess her had spiked his passion to a level he hadn't been able to control.

He felt as if he had lost part of himself during the process. Part of his heart and soul. He'd given it to Sarah.

That had never happened to him before.

He'd also forgotten protection.

That had never happened before, either.

In fact, in the heat of their joining, he'd even imagined putting his baby in Sarah's belly. The two of them making a life together, a family.

Afraid he was crushing her, he slowly lifted himself from her and slid to her side. She rolled over instantly, threw her arm across his chest and snuggled in his arms. He should pull away, talk to her right now, but she tangled her legs with his, and he lost his ability to speak.

The storm had ended outside, yet tomorrow another one might brew—one of a different kind. Unable to resist a few more hours with her before they were torn apart by what had happened to his sister, he cradled her in his arms, brushed a kiss on the top of her hair and held her, emotions for her spilling over as they both fell asleep.

SARAH WOKE in the early hours of the morning, faint sunbeams creating shadows in the cave and dappling Adam's handsome face with hazy light. She loved him more than she'd ever thought possible. He'd treated her like a whole woman the night before, not as if she were fragile or inadequate.

Maybe they could have a life together once this whole ordeal was over.

Beautiful sounds filled her head now—the husky whisper of his voice saying her name when he'd climbed on top of her. The echo of his breath in the

cave. The trickle of a waterfall inside the cave somewhere in the distance.

Love for him swelled in her heart. She could no
longer deny her feelings or that she wanted to be with
him.

She'd wanted to cry out his name in the throes of
passion, to murmur erotic words to him the way he
had done to her during the night. She opened her
mouth, wanting to whisper her love, wanting to wake
him with the sound of her voice.

The stunning reality of that thought made her
pause. Could she speak if she wanted? It had been so
many years, would her speech sound childlike and
garbled? Had she let her fears keep her a prisoner of
silence all these years?

Lifting a hand to trace his bare chest, she felt the
familiar stir of heat and desire rise within her. Now
that daylight dawned, would he love her the way he
had the night before? No. They needed to move on.
To find Denise.

She stared at his features, memorizing each one—
the hard planes and angles of his face, the way his
lips parted in sleep, the way his broad shoulders and
strong arms held her tightly, the puckered scar on the
lower left side near his shoulder, the thick hair on his
chest, tapering down to cup his sex, the strong muscles in his thighs and calves.

She swallowed, summoning the courage to say his
name, when his eyes slowly opened. Dark lashes
framed the near-black irises as he scrubbed his hand
across his beard-stubbled jaw. But his expression
reeked of regret, dousing water on the flame of her
desire, and her courage waned.

And somewhere in the back of her mind, she heard

the distinct sound of Denise crying again. This time the sound haunted her, the low cry sounding frail and weak as if she had given up.

"WE SHOULDN'T HAVE done that," Adam said, bracing himself for the disappointment he'd find in Sarah's eyes when he distanced himself this morning. But he had to distance himself. Last night, he'd gotten too damn close.

He'd almost lost his heart.

Something a good cop couldn't do or he'd get sidetracked and mess up.

She arched a fine brow, wariness in her eyes, then mouthed, "No."

"No, what? No, it wasn't a mistake?" Anger got the better of him as he moved away from her and stood. "Yes, it was, Sarah. For God's sakes, us being together, it's just the danger, the tension. We both needed a release."

She flinched as if he'd slapped her and he realized he must sound cold, reducing their lovemaking to a physical need for release, but he couldn't tell her the truth.

That he cared about her. That deep down inside, he wondered if he could make a relationship work, if she could be his wife and have his child. If they could lead a normal life.

But he didn't know what normal was anymore. Another woman had died because he'd let his emotions sidetrack him from his job. Could he live with himself if he allowed that to happen again? And even if he did want Sarah, what could he offer her?

There were things he'd wanted when he was little, material things his family couldn't afford, things Denise had wanted that they couldn't pay for. Could he ask a child to understand that?

And what about security? It had been painful enough for him losing his parents as a teen. His job put him in danger every day—could he chance putting a son or daughter through that kind of life, where they never knew if their father would come home alive at night?

No, he couldn't.

"Look, if you're fantasizing about us having some kind of normal life, then think again. Cops make lousy money and even lousier husbands."

She bit down on her lip.

"My job is my life, and it's too damn dangerous for a woman like you to be involved with. We need to get going."

He ignored the hurt in her expressive eyes.

"And there's no telling what we might find today, Sarah. If your father is alive, or if your godfather had something to do with Denise's disappearance, I'll have to take them down."

He grabbed his clothes and yanked on his jeans, unable to look at her naked body, the one he'd loved so thoroughly the night before.

"We need to hurry to get there before daylight," he said.

He gritted his teeth when she reached for her clothes, and began to dress without arguing.

"See," he said, bitterness filling his voice. "You can't even talk to me. You're afraid to, aren't you, Sarah? You don't trust me enough, right? Just like you didn't trust me enough to tell me about the article. What kind of relationship is that?"

She jerked her clothes on, hurt shimmering in her tear-misted eyes.

He turned away, knowing her silent surrender in the night had proven the opposite, that she did trust him, at least with her body. That they didn't need words to communicate.

Chapter Twenty-Two

Sarah fought the hurt coursing through her at Adam's dismissal. He'd accused her of being afraid. Last night, she'd sensed his need; his hunger for her went deeper than the physical. She'd sensed he was the one afraid, too afraid to get involved, too afraid to let himself love her.

Maybe she was wrong. After all, she was inexperienced, her own emotions swirling in a tailspin.

Adam had so much on his mind right now, she couldn't add to his problems by acting like a helpless woman.

Maybe she would prove to him today that she wasn't helpless. And hopefully, they could find Denise and end the pain of Denise's cries ringing in her ears.

Squaring her shoulders, she fastened the last button on her blouse, accepted the bottle of water and granola bar from Adam and ate it in silence. He downed a snack also, then glanced at her, a wariness in his face that mirrored her own feelings.

No matter what had happened between them, they both wanted to see his sister alive.

"Sarah?"

She hesitated, wiping her mouth with her hand.

"I forgot to use protection last night," his voice dropped. "I...if anything happens, let me know, okay?"

Anger slammed into her. They were communicating just fine—in fact, his message came through loud and clear. He'd take care of his responsibilities. Well, she didn't want to be a responsibility. She wanted him to love her.

Maybe that was impossible.

Her own father certainly hadn't loved her. How could a strong man like Adam?

He gave her a last tortured look. "Are you ready?"

She nodded angrily, then followed him outside.

THEY'D PROBABLY HIKED a mile across the island, past two security stands when the first shot rang out. Adam ducked, grabbed Sarah's hand and began to run. Dodging bullets, they wove in and out of the thick brush, Adam's heart pounding.

Another bullet zinged above their heads and he pulled Sarah into a thicket of trees, crouching down and waiting. Seconds later, footsteps pounded the sand, two male voices breaking the silence.

"Which way did they go?"

"I think they're headed toward Building A."

The footsteps came closer. Adam tore off a vine and stuck it out just as the two approached. The first man sprawled into the brush, the second let loose a round from a semiautomatic. Adam slammed him on the head with the butt of his gun. The man sputtered, then rolled back unconscious. The second man ran up shooting, and Adam tackled him. They struggled, fighting for the guard's gun, shots flying across the area, but Adam managed to karate chop him in the shoulder blades, then he knocked him unconscious.

Sarah grabbed a vine and helped him tie the men's hands behind their backs. Adam dragged them into the brush, secured them to a tree, disarming them and throwing the machine-gun strap over his shoulder.

"Let's go."

He grabbed Sarah's hand and lead her along, crossing the sandy terrain and weaving their way past another guard's post until they reached the middle of the island.

There, amidst the shadow of a cluster of live oaks, sat the building where Sarah's father had conducted his research. It was supposedly empty for renovation, but Adam saw a small light burning in the back of the building. Someone was inside.

He urged Sarah forward. But he froze when the blunt end of a gun pressed into his back.

The minute Adam spun around, his high kick connected with the guard's gun. Sarah hit the ground in a dive. She covered her head with her hands and crawled to the building, dodging a spray of bullets as the gun soared through the air, releasing the first round.

Adam slammed his fist into the man's face, sending him to his knees, then quickly knocked him unconscious. Pulse hammering, he ran to her.

"Hurry, let's get inside."

Thankfully, since the building was in the midst of renovation, the security system hadn't been updated. Adam slipped inside, surveying the space, holding Sarah behind him. A wide room, obviously meant as a reception area, occupied the front with two long corridors to each side which he assumed would house offices and labs. The building had three floors but the dark rooms and lack of noise indicated they were empty.

Sarah crouched behind Adam, making as little sound as possible while he traveled down the first hall. Muffled voices drifted through the vacant space.

Adam pointed to the opposite corridor, and they inched through a hallway separating the two, scanning each room, but found nothing.

Finally, footsteps tapped on the hard linoleum floor from the back room. Sarah's breath caught.

"Hell, where are they?" a man's voice bellowed. "Dammit, find them and kill them. We've come too far to let everything blow up in our faces now!"

Sarah tensed at the sound of the voice. She'd heard the same husky timbre in the hospital, she was almost sure of it. But who did the voice belong to?

"Yes, sir," a second voice said in a clipped tone.

Footsteps clicked on the hard floor, echoing in the silence. Adam motioned for her to stay behind him, pulled out his gun, and they headed toward the sounds.

ADAM SCANNED the long hallway. Offices were housed on the front end, two separate labs on the back. They had to be holding Denise there.

That is, *if* they had her.

Moving slowly, he prayed he hadn't made a mistake in bringing Sarah. A guard paced in front of the lab, armed and looking anxious. Only one guard?

He watched for several seconds, searching for the second man, but didn't see him. He motioned for Sarah to stay put, crept forward, then lunged at the guard and took him out.

Seconds later, he grabbed the guard's keys and unlocked the door. When he opened the door, the scent
of alcohol and drugs assaulted him. A single dim light
hung in the center of the vacant lab room, but in the
corner on a low cot, he finally found his sister.

Chapter Twenty-Three

Sarah gasped at the sight of Denise's pale face. She was lying so still, her arms tied down, her eyes closed. Was she alive?

Adam raced to her side and quickly checked her breathing. Relief filled his face when he turned to Sarah. "She's got a pulse, but she's been drugged."

Sarah struggled to untie Denise's arms while Adam gently patted her face. "Denise, honey, it's me, Adam. Can you hear me?"

Sarah's stomach convulsed when she didn't respond.

"Denise, sweetie, wake up, we've got to get you out of here."

Adam took over one arm and Sarah worked the other until they freed her hands. Sarah undid her feet while Adam curved his arm around Denise's waist to help her sit up.

"Denise, wake up. We've got to leave."

Slowly, her eyes opened, looking dazed as she stared at her brother.

"Adam?"

"Yeah, honey. We're going to get you out of here."

"They—they want my research," Denise mumbled, slowly looking from Adam to Sarah.

"I know, honey. Who did this to you?"

"Tried to call for help," Denise said, her words slurring. "In the hospital."

"I know, sweetie." Adam gestured toward Sarah. "This is Sarah Cutter. She heard you call out. We've been looking for you ever since." Emotions caught in his voice and he dragged Denise into his arms. She hugged him back, collapsing against his chest she was so weak. Sarah swallowed back tears, thanking God that Denise was still alive.

Adam finally pulled back and brushed Denise's tangled brown hair from her face. "Can you stand up, sis?"

Denise frowned. "I think so. What happened?"

"They drugged you. I need you to tell me everyone involved just as soon as we escape the island."

"Island?"

"Yeah, they've been holding you in a vacant building on Nighthawk Island."

Adam helped her slide from the bed, placing his arm around her waist for support. Sarah fell into place on the other side, draping Denise's arm over her shoulder to help. Together they walked toward the door, Denise's feet dragging on the linoleum.

"Have to change the research," Denise mumbled, pulling to a stop. "They told me to finish it here in seclusion, that a foreign government was after it, so they had to take me away."

"But they drugged you at the hospital?"

"They told me a foreign agent tried to kidnap me, but Seaside Securities stopped them. At least that's what they said. They claimed they brought me here to protect me while I finished the research.''

"They lied," Adam said. "And after you finished, they planned to kill you."

"I can't believe they'd do this," Denise whispered.

"Believe it, sis. It's not the first time, either. A microbiologist named Jerome Simms died suspiciously four years ago. A week later, the center announced a major sale."

"But why? I wouldn't personally profit from selling my work?"

"My guess is that a competitor was working on something similar, and time was running out. So they decided to sell to a foreign market."

"They didn't want to wait on U.S. clinical trials," Denise said, her voice stronger. "The foreign government doesn't have as stringent requirements."

Adam nodded.

"I got suspicious," Denise admitted, rubbing at her head. "I started asking questions a couple of days ago, that's the last thing I remember."

"They drugged you. I'm so sorry, Neesie."

"I have to change the research," Denise said, looking more alert as she surveyed her surroundings. "I can't let it fall into the wrong hands."

"We will, but let's get out of here."

"No, the computer, help me to the computer over there."

Adam hesitated, but Denise seemed so insistent, he finally helped her to the computer in the corner of the lab.

He stood over her shoulder while she accessed the files. Data spilled onto the screen, but his sister typed in several commands, quickly going through several pages of notes. Adam headed to the door to watch out, but before he made it, footsteps clicked outside. Two guards appeared at the door.

"Stop it right there, Dr. Harley. You're all going with us."

Adam gave Sarah a pain-filled look as the men aimed their guns at them, hauled them up and out the door.

Several tense minutes later, the guards ordered them to climb aboard a cruiser, then guided them into a small cabin.

Sarah gasped when Sol and Arnold Hughes walked in, looking furious.

"You just couldn't leave things alone, could you, Sarah?" Sol swiped at the perspiration trickling down his jaw, his eyes ablaze with anger. "I begged you to stay out of this, to let it rest."

Sarah stared at him in shock. No, she couldn't believe it. Surely, Sol hadn't done something as sinister as orchestrating Denise's kidnapping.

Arnold Hughes gestured toward her godfather to sit down, aiming his gun at Sol. Sol was shaking, fear etched on his face as he dropped into a wooden chair by the table.

ADAM'S STOMACH CLENCHED at the pain on Sarah's face. "So, you two were behind this whole thing?" Adam asked, hoping to stall long enough to come up with a plan for escape.

"The center needed the money," Hughes said in a cold voice. "It was nothing personal, simply business."

"It was my sister's life," Adam said through gritted teeth.

"And other people's," Denise added. "My work is not complete. It needs clinical trials."

"We don't have time for that, not with a competitor one step ahead. This was our only chance to get the sale." Hughes's hand tightened around the .38.

"Greed," Adam said, shooting Sol a look of disdain. "And here you preached all that moralistic stuff about your research, wanting to help the world."

"We do." Sol rammed a nervous hand through his thinning hair. "But we have to consider the bigger picture."

"And Jerome Simms—I suppose he didn't fit into that picture?"

"That was a most unfortunate accident," Hughes said with a leer. He turned to Denise. "And if your brother hadn't started asking questions and raising suspicions all over the place, and Ms. Cutter hadn't butted her nose into things, there wouldn't be any need for this to end this way."

Denise raised her chin defiantly. "What do you mean?"

"We never intended to kill you, Dr. Harley. We only planned to alter your memory," Hughes explained.

"You were going to let me return to my work?"

"Essentially you wouldn't have remembered anything about this project, but your mind would still be intact for others." Hughes grinned, the mole at the corner of his lip jerking with the movement. "You really are a good scientist, Dr. Harley. It will be a shame to see you go."

"Sarah, if you'd only left it alone. I'm so sorry," Sol said in a low sorrowful voice.

Sarah lifted her hand and signed, her jerky movements a testament to her anger.

"No, baby, I didn't try to have you killed." Sol's face paled. "I would never hurt you. I—" he hesitated, tears choking his voice "—I found out Hughes hired someone to kill you, so I tried to get you to stop asking questions so he'd call him off. And I—I set up Gates to die, hoping you'd drop things."

"You killed Gates?" Adam asked.

"Donny's dead?" Denise clung to his arm, and Adam covered her hand with his.

Sol nodded. "I didn't kill him."

"But you hired someone," Adam concluded. "Did Gates really have a fixation with my sister or did you make that up, too?"

Sol glanced toward Hughes as if he knew they'd gone too far, but he hadn't been able to stop things from snowballing. "He had a crush on her, yes, but as far as being obsessed...no."

They needed to let Gates's mother know, Adam thought, remembering her anguished cries when they'd removed her son's body.

Sarah caught Sol's attention again and began to sign. Adam knew she was hurting and wanted to comfort her, but he had to focus on an escape plan. Hopefully, Russell would have called Clay by now and backup would be on its way.

"Let's go." Hughes motioned toward Santenelli.

"No, first, I have to tell Sarah the truth," Santenelli said. "She deserves to know about her father."

THE AIR IN Sarah's lungs tightened. "Is my father still alive?"

"No." Sol said. "He died in the fire that day."

Santenelli moved toward Sarah but she backed away, practically melting into the seat to avoid his touch. Exhaling wearily, Santenelli pulled at his chin. "But he wasn't a traitor. He never intended to sell his device to the Russians."

Relief surged through Sarah, followed by an ache that there was no hope her dad was still alive.

"Your father loved you, Sarah. He didn't kill your mother." Santenelli's voice broke as he glanced at Hughes. Sarah understood the message—Hughes had killed her parents. "When your father found out about our plans to sell the device, he was furious. He tried to persuade us not to sell, but we'd already given a verbal agreement."

"There was a lot of money involved," Hughes interjected. "Your father was a fool."

"So you framed him?" Adam asked, his hand reaching down to squeeze Sarah's icy one in his own.

Santenelli nodded. "We hired a man to set the explosion. You and your mom weren't supposed to be home that day, but you had a cold so your mom didn't go out." Santenelli paced across the small room. "The bomb went off just as your father arrived home. I didn't want your mother to die, Sarah, you have to believe me, I loved her. When I learned she was in there, that you were... God, I couldn't stand it. I thought I would die, too."

"That's the reason you never married," Sarah signed, recognizing the truth by the tortured look in her godfather's eyes.

"Yes," Sol said, choking with tears. "And your father tried to get in to save you but..."

"But what?" Sarah signed.

"But I got rid of him," Hughes announced, waving

the gun. "Now, it's time to finish up this little true confessions."

"Wait, explain one more thing," Adam said. "How could Sarah hear my sister?"

"The hearing implant," Sol admitted. "We developed it from the hearing device her father had worked on. Recently we revamped the technology. The guard watching Denise was wearing one of the devices." He paused for a breath. "In developing the hearing implant for Sarah, some small part of the transmitter must have been left intact so you heard things sporadically. Like a radio transmitter."

Sarah blinked back the tears, oblivious to Sol's explanation as anger at Arnold Hughes churned through her. He had robbed her of her father, her mother, her whole life because of money. She hated him, she hated everything he'd done. Pain swept through her, fueling her fury. She lunged at Hughes, throwing her fists at him.

"No, Sarah!" Adam pulled her away, and the guards rushed in, waving their guns.

"You're not going to kill Sarah!" Sol suddenly jumped Hughes.

Then the sound of a gunshot exploded into the air.

Chapter Twenty-Four

Everything happened at once. Sol clutched his chest, blood spurting out as he fell to the floor with a strangled groan. Sarah cried out in anguish and dove for him while Adam struggled with the guard. The other guard held Denise, his weapon aimed at her head.

Sarah pressed her hands over Sol's bloody ones, his eyelids fluttering.

"So sorry, Sarah," he whispered in a pain-filled voice.

Sarah's heart ached, confusion tangling with her emotions.

"Just know that your father loved you, Sarah." His breathing rasped out, and Sarah realized he was going to die. There was nothing she could do. There was so much blood, seeping through his fingers, running down his crisp white shirt. "And I did, too, I—I tried to make up for all of it. To be your family."

Tears clogged Sarah's throat as he took his last breath, and his eyes glazed over into the fixed stare of death.

Behind her, she heard Adam struggling and turned to see the guard slam him to the floor. She jumped up to help, but Hughes caught her, just as the guard knocked Adam unconscious.

"Tie them up. We'll burn the boat and let the sharks finish them."

"You'll never get away with this," Denise yelled, struggling against the guard's hold. "And even when you do, I altered my research. So it's not worth anything to you."

Hughes simply smiled as if she was wrong, then turned and left the guards to follow his orders.

SEVERAL MINUTES LATER, Sarah and Denise fought against their bindings. Sol's dead body lay in the corner, Adam's unconscious one bound between them.

The scent of gasoline permeated her nostrils, the strong stench of wood and fiberglass beginning to burn. Someone had set fire to the deck. It would only take seconds to reach the cabin. They were really doing it, Sarah thought in horror. They would kill them all, then cover up their crimes just as they had done when they'd framed her father.

Fury swept through her, a rage more potent because of the things Hughes had actually made her believe about her own father. Her parents' deaths, Sol's, all so senseless. All because of money.

Gritting her teeth, she dug her fingernails into her palms and maneuvered her chair nearer Denise. Denise did the same, trying to talk behind her gag. Several tense seconds later, they struggled to untie one another, the sizzle of the fire crackling along with their labored breathing.

Finally Sarah felt the knot loosen. She slipped the ropes free, then worked to untie her feet.

Fire sprang up outside the glass window, the flames

leaping toward the doorway. Sarah froze. They would have to go through the fire.

Memories assaulted her, paralyzing her with fear. *She could see her mother in the doorway, the fire consuming her, melting her clothes, her skin.... Her father was on the other side, pulling at the door. Yes, he was going to save them. Then pain slammed into her....*

A sob tore from her, deep and anguished.

"Sarah, hurry, we have to get out of here!"

Denise's frightened voice broke through the haze, jerking Sarah back to the moment. To Adam, the man she loved. The only person in the world she had left to care about.

She jumped into motion and dropped down beside Denise, tearing at the ropes on his hands as Denise untied his feet. Adam moaned, his eyes remained closed. Fire clawed at the door, smoke seeping below the narrow space below it. Sarah ran to the door and tried to open it, but heat scalded her hand. Panicking, she searched the room for some other way to escape, but they were trapped.

"We have to open that door," Denise said.

Sarah checked beneath the sink and found a fire extinguisher. She hurried to the door and tried to smash the wood. Seconds later, the door cracked. She opened the fire extinguisher and sprayed, dousing the worst of the flames from the door to clear them a path. Frantic, she ran to Adam, and helped Denise drag him toward the door. The fire caught onto the wooden edges and rippled inside the cabin in small patches, sizzling and taking on a life of its own.

"On the count of three, we go, and go fast!" Denise shouted.

Sarah nodded while Denise counted. "Three!"

Heat seared Sarah, her body sweating as she and Denise hurriedly dragged Adam through the blaze, across the deck. Fire clawed at her feet, and a small flame caught Adam's shirt, but Denise quickly slapped it out with her hand. Finally they reached the edge, cool air hit them and Adam stirred.

"We have to get off the boat, Adam, it's on fire!" Denise yelled.

He moaned and pushed up onto his knees. The fire blazed closer behind them, the sound of wood popping rent the air.

"It's getting to the gas, the boat's going to blow," Adam mumbled. "Jump!"

Sarah and Denise grabbed his arms and they leaped to the dock just before the boat exploded behind them.

THE FORCE OF the explosion rocked the dock, and Adam threw his arms over Sarah and Denise, trying to shield them from flying debris. Burning fiberglass and splintered pieces of the boat pelted the dock and sailed into the water. Sarah's body quaked beneath him, his sister's hands clawed his arms.

He quickly checked to see if they'd been injured and helped them both stand. The fear in Sarah's eyes hit him like a punch in the gut. But it wasn't fear for herself, he realized, it was fear for him. He desperately wanted to pull her into his arms and hold her, to tell her it was all right, but there wasn't time.

"We have to get to Clay," he said gruffly.

"You're not going anywhere." One of the guards from Seaside Securities stood over them. Hughes aimed the gun at Adam.

Sarah flinched, and Adam saw the fierce determination in her eyes as she lunged toward Hughes. She wasn't going to let Arnold Hughes kill any more of the people she loved. Adam pushed her aside, but Hughes fired the gun.

Just as the bullet ricocheted through the air, Adam heard Sarah shout his name.

Chapter Twenty-Five

Pain shot through Adam's shoulder at the bullet's impact, but he ignored it, fear paralyzing him when Hughes slammed Sarah to the ground.

A loud rumbling sound suddenly filled the air. Hughes ran from the dock, jumped onto another boat and took off.

The thunderous roar grew louder. A helicopter.

A man's voice barreled through a bullhorn. "Freeze. Police. Put down your weapons."

Clay. Thank God he'd arrived.

Suddenly the helicopter landed, Clay and Bernstein and several other officers charged the area, taking control, putting an APB out on Hughes. Russell jumped from the chopper and swept Denise into his arms. Adam raced over to Sarah, his heart clenching at her crumpled form.

He felt a slow pulse beating, but blood spurted from her head and as he pulled her into his lap, more blood seeped from her ear. "We need a doctor," Adam yelled above the noise. "We have to get her to the emergency room now!"

The next four hours were the longest of Adam's life. He'd barely been able to endure being treated for the gunshot wound for wanting to be with Sarah. The bullet had torn through his shoulder and exited the other side, but he hadn't needed surgery. Sarah had.

He jammed the pain pills in his pocket, refusing to take them because he wanted to be coherent when Sarah woke. He paced the waiting room, praying like he'd never prayed in his life.

She'd gotten hurt because she'd been trying to save him. And Denise. And she'd called out his name.

He should have saved her.

"Adam, stop beating yourself up," Denise said, lifting a hand to massage his shoulder.

He shook his head, wondering how she'd read his mind. Russell remained seated on the vinyl couch in the corner, his gaze never leaving Denise. Adam had no doubt about his brother-in-law now. The second Russell hugged his sister, Adam had known Russell really loved her.

"I know you're blaming yourself because I know you," Denise said quietly. She pulled his hands into hers and faced him. "But you're not to blame here. You saved me, and you probably saved Sarah's life at the end."

"It wasn't enough," Adam muttered. "She shouldn't have been hurt." And she'd screamed his name to save him. The first time he'd heard her speak, the first time she'd said his name—it had almost gotten her killed.

Guilt tore through him. How could he have accused her of being afraid? She was the most courageous woman he'd ever met.

"She seems tough, Adam, she'll survive."

The other woman, Pamela, hadn't.

"You want to tell me what happened between the two of you?"

Adam winced, but shook his head. "It's complicated."

"You're in love with her, aren't you?"

Adam froze. He had never let himself think about love. Love hurt too much. Having a family and losing it had been too painful. He couldn't go through that again.

"Okay, so you won't admit it, but you are. And she loves you, too, Adam. I saw it in her eyes when you were unconscious and we dragged you through the fire."

"It doesn't matter," Adam said. "My job is my life, Denise, you know that. You of all people should understand it, too."

"Yeah, I do." Denise emitted a self-deprecating laugh. "When I was all alone with my work in that lab, I realized something, Adam. All my adult life I'd poured myself into my job, claiming I wanted to save the world, but I was really hiding behind my work." Denise paused. "I was afraid of loving too deeply, of having that family I really wanted torn from me like it was when Mom and Dad died."

His sister's words mirrored his own emotions so closely he couldn't respond.

"But when I was alone and thought I might not ever have the chance to get my life back," Denise said, "I realized I didn't want to hide any more. I wasn't going to let fear stand in my way."

"So, you're not going through with the divorce?"

"Russell risked his life and his career to help save me." Denise gave her husband a secretive look, one that reminded Adam of the silent bond between him and Sarah, the one that was so precious and tentative. "I want to have that family with him now," Denise continued. "Work is work, Adam, but it doesn't keep you warm at night, and it won't keep you company when you're old. Don't be afraid to go after Sarah if you love her."

"It's not the same," Adam said. "I let another woman interfere with my job once, a witness, and she died." He explained about the incident with Pamela.

"Give yourself a chance, Adam. Mom and Dad would want you to be happy, not to work all the time to avenge their deaths."

Adam agreed to think about what she'd said. Denise brushed a kiss on his temple and stood, going back to Russell. Clay's voice brought his head up.

"Hey, partner. Any word yet?"

Adam cleared his throat. "No. What happened with Hughes? Is he in custody?"

Clay sat down, one hand curled around a cup of coffee. "Crashed his boat into the jetty. Haven't found his body yet. Divers are searching, but the tide was bad, so it may have washed out to sea."

Adam grimaced. He didn't like loose ends. But if the sharks finished Hughes off, it would be good enough for him.

"We matched the prints in Sarah's house with one of the security guards. He admitted Hughes paid him to off Sarah. He was the one who broke into her apartment and ran her off the road. We've got him in custody."

Adam nodded. He would make sure the man paid.

The doctor entered the waiting room and cleared his throat. "Does Ms. Cutter have any family here?"

"No, no family," Adam said, hating how empty

and alone Sarah would feel without Sol. "But you can tell me about her condition." He identified himself. Denise and Russell gathered close.

"I'm Dr. Eugene Hall, chief surgeon here. I'm afraid things didn't go as well as we'd hoped."

Adam's gut clenched. "She didn't..." He couldn't even say it.

"She made it through the surgery and she'll be all right." The doctor worried the pocket of his lab coat.

"What is it, then?" Adam asked. "What's wrong?"

"The hearing implant," Hall said, his face tight with concern. "We had to remove it. The trauma to the head was too much, it caused internal damage, swelling. We were worried about the possibility of infection which could lead to the brain." He shook his head sadly. "I'm sorry. Maybe in a few months after she's had time to heal, she might be able to receive another one. We'll just have to wait and see."

The room grew dark around Adam, sucking him into some kind of surreal state. After all Sarah had lost, she was going to lose her hearing again. She'd be cruelly thrust back into that silent world where she'd lived all alone.

And it was all his fault.

"Can I see her?"

"She's still in recovery."

Adam gripped the man's arm. "Please, doctor..."

"Okay, but just for a minute."

His heart heavy, Adam followed the doctor to the recovery room. The scent of hospital antiseptics and medicine surrounded him, the IV and tubes attached to Sarah a cold reality. She was lying so still, the crisp white sheets tucked around her, her face deathly pale.

A small bandage had been wound around her head, but it was the internal damage that had been so scary. She'd wanted to hear for twenty years, but she'd lost that ability less than a month after receiving the implant.

All because of him.

She was so beautiful with her hair spilling around her, her dainty lips parted slightly in sleep, her slender hands limp on top of the sheet. He took her hand in his and squeezed it, hoping the warmth of his body could erase the chill in her hands.

"Sarah, I'm so sorry," he whispered, knowing she couldn't hear him. Knowing that even if she were awake, she wouldn't be able to.

He'd failed her. He'd dragged her into his life, used her to find his sister, then hadn't protected her when she'd needed it the most. What would happen to her when she awoke and realized she couldn't hear? Would she hate him?

He didn't think he could bear it if she did. Not after the way she'd looked at him with love in her eyes when he'd made love to her. But he didn't deserve her love. And he couldn't ask her forgiveness.

"I—" he leaned over and brushed his lips across hers "—I love you."

He knew she hadn't heard him, but he turned and walked out the door, knowing in his heart that she'd be better off without him.

FIRE BLAZED around Sarah, teasing her, hissing at her that it would get her next. Adam lay in the middle of the blaze, smoke curling around his face. No!

They had to get out. She had to rescue him.

But her eyes were so heavy, she couldn't open

them. Pain splintered through her head, ringing in her ears, and a strange numbness had settled inside her temple. Where was she?

Slowly, she lifted her lids. Fear gripped her. She would see the fire again, the flames.

No. It was gone. Everything was white. No colors, no bright orange of the blaze.

Adam.

Where was he?

He had whispered that he loved her.

Or had she been dreaming?

She opened her mouth and said his name, searching the empty room. But he was nowhere to be found.

A doctor entered the room. White coat, stethoscope, a concerned look drawn on his face. He opened his mouth to speak and his mouth moved.

But there was only silence.

Chapter Twenty-Six

The next two days passed in a blur for Sarah. She slept and rested and struggled to adjust to the truth about Sol, about her past, about losing the implant.

She would survive.

She had before and she would now. At least she knew this time that her father had loved her, that he had died trying to rescue her and her mother. That knowledge alone and the fact that she'd helped find Adam's sister was worth all she'd been through the past few days.

But she missed Adam desperately.

She wouldn't beg him to see her or to accept her imperfections.

Still, she finished dressing, grateful that one of the nurses had brought her a denim skirt and a blouse to wear home, and looked out the window, waiting on the taxi, absorbing the quietness around her and letting the peacefulness seep into her.

Seconds later, she felt a tap on her arm and her heart catapulted.

She spun around, hoping it was Adam.

Denise stood in front of her instead.

She tried to mask her disappointment, but she could

tell by the sympathetic look on his sister's face that she understood. Odd, how she felt such a kinship with this woman and she barely knew her.

Denise handed her a letter. Sarah accepted the rose-printed stationery, and sat down on the edge of the bed.

Dear Sarah,

There aren't words to express how thankful I am to you for all you did to help Adam find me. If you hadn't come forth, he might not have realized that I was in trouble until it was too late. I'm so terribly sorry that you were hurt saving me, that you lost your hearing again. I hope we can be friends.

I don't know for sure what happened between you and Adam, but he's a good man. He's done so much for me, he deserves some happiness. He took out loans to put me through school, and he's still paying them back. That's why he lives in that crummy apartment.

Anyway, I hope things work out for you. If there's anything I can ever do for you, please let me know.

                                        Sincerely,
                                        Denise.

Tears pricked at Sarah's eyes, but she blinked them away. She knew Adam was a good man. Now she understood why he lived in that apartment, too. But he wasn't coming to see her. He didn't want a family, ties, especially to someone he'd see as needy. He'd spent his life taking care of others.

She had to let him go.

She scribbled a note to Denise. "I'd love to be friends. And please don't worry about me, I'll be okay. I'm going to return to my teaching soon. Meanwhile I'm going to clear my father's name. That's all the thanks I need from you."

"I want you to come to my wedding," Denise wrote. "Russell and I are going to renew our vows."

Sarah smiled and nodded.

"For what it's worth," Denise wrote, "my brother loves you. I just hope he wakes up one day and realizes it."

Sarah's heart was breaking. She'd wanted that, too. But it wasn't going to happen.

ADAM LISTENED to his sister and her husband restate their wedding vows. He'd never seen his sister so happy and alive as she'd been the last two weeks.

He'd never felt more dead inside himself.

He hadn't seen or spoken to Sarah.

Denise had said she'd invited her to the ceremony, but Sarah hadn't shown. He knew it was because of him. Because he hadn't had the courage to face her.

How could he look into Sarah's face, say her name and know that it was his fault she couldn't hear?

"You may kiss the bride," the reverend said.

Russell and Denise embraced, a long kiss following that made Adam yearn to hold Sarah in his arms, to feel her lips against his, to know that they could have a future together like his sister and her husband did.

A few minutes later, he joined the reception to congratulate them. His sister's gaze darted around the room.

"I was hoping Sarah would come."

Adam shrugged. "I'm sorry, sis."

"You should be." A hint of anger tinged her voice. "She probably didn't come just to avoid you."

"Can you blame her?" Adam asked. "I'm the reason she lost her hearing again."

Denise jabbed her finger in his chest. "You're the stupidest, most stubborn man I know. For heaven's sake, Adam, stop thinking the whole world rests on your shoulders."

"I don't—"

"Shut up and listen." Denise glared at him. "Sarah is the most courageous woman I've ever met. She could be home feeling sorry for herself or giving up on life, but she's not. She's out there working again, clearing her father's name and missing you."

"How do you know she misses me?"

Denise rolled her eyes. "Because I just do. And she probably thinks you don't want her because she can't hear."

"What?"

"That's right, brother dear."

"That's ridiculous, I—"

"You love her, don't be a coward, go ahead and say it."

Adam shrugged. "So, maybe I do."

"Then go tell her."

ADAM WATCHED Sarah through the glass window at her school, her assistant, Adrianne, by his side interpreting. Sarah raised her hands and introduced the song to the children. "This is a special song that a friend of mine wrote.

> Silent cries of anger
> silent cries of hurt

were all wrapped up inside
the words that no one heard.

The kids watched intently, mimicking her. "What do you think the words mean?" she asked.

One little boy raised his hand and signed. "That someone hurts too much to talk about what's bothering them."

Sarah nodded. "That's right. When you're hurting inside, it's better to tell someone. So, if you ever need to talk, you know you can come to me."

Had Sarah realized he'd written the song about himself, about the pain and guilt he'd buried inside?

She had saved his life because she'd had the courage to shout out his name. He should have the courage to be honest with her. He had to go to her and tell her how he felt.

He turned to Adrianne. "I need some help," he finally said.

SARAH HUGGED the last child and waved goodbye. She loved her job. She loved the kids.

And one day she wanted to have some of her own.

A little boy with dark hair and dark eyes...

Her heart wrenched, the dull ache she'd lived with the last two weeks steady. When would it go away? When would she stop wanting Adam Black?

She could see his tall handsome figure, his black hair, those dark eyes so intensely studying her. The image was so vivid it was almost real.

She shook herself, thinking the figure she'd seen through the glass was a product of her imagination when suddenly the image disappeared. Her heart sank. Only seconds later, it skipped a beat again when he materialized in the doorway.

He was beautiful.

Breathtakingly handsome in a black suit and blue shirt.

He'd come from Denise's ceremony, she realized. The one she had missed because she hadn't thought she could stand seeing Adam and not touching him.

"Sarah."

She saw his mouth move and read his lips. But the tense silence reminded her that she might never hear his husky voice again. And that her impairment was one of the reasons she could never be with him.

"Can we go somewhere and talk?"

She stared at his mouth, aching to touch it, to touch him. To hold him.

"Please. There are some things I have to say to you."

She hesitated, then shrugged, helpless to say no when it meant being close to him one more time.

They crossed the sidewalk in silence, then strolled over to River Street and walked along the river. Spring flowers bloomed, dotting the park with their color, the luscious scents of their fragrances perfuming the air. A few pigeons swooped down to gather crumbs from picnickers, kids played on the playground, and a long-haired guy sat strumming the guitar beneath a live oak. Sarah remembered the time Adam had played for her and smiled.

He finally paused at a picnic bench facing the Savannah River and she sat down, twining her hands in her lap.

Sun slanted off his features, highlighting his wide cheekbones and his dark eyes. She tried to read his expression, but the tingling attraction that had splintered through her the moment she'd seen him clouded her mind.

"The wedding was beautiful. I wish you'd come."

She arched a brow, waiting on him to elaborate.

"Denise wanted to see you."

Disappointment tugged at her.

"I—I wanted you to be there, too."

Hope slipped inside.

"Can you forgive me for what happened at the island? For you losing your hearing?"

She frowned and shook her head. He had to know that wasn't his fault.

He reached out and tugged her hand into his. "Sarah, I'm sorry for everything that happened. I—"

He suddenly released her hand and began to sign.

It was now or never, Adam thought, his courage shaky. The moment he'd seen Sarah in the room with those kids he'd known he wanted her to be his wife.

"Please forgive me for what happened on the island."

She shook her head again.

"Yes, I'll spend the rest of my life making it up to you."

She took a pad and pencil and scratched a note. "I don't want your apologies or your pity, Adam. You didn't cause me to lose my hearing. Arnold Hughes did. And Sol." She paused to give him a meaningful glance. "I would gladly go through that again to have learned that my father loved me, that he died trying to save me instead of trying to kill me. And I'm not an invalid, I don't need anyone taking care of me. I can take care of myself."

She didn't blame him? Didn't hate him?

No, she didn't, he realized, as he looked deep into her eyes. In fact, he saw a sort of peace there, one he hadn't seen before. Maybe knowing her father had loved her was enough.

Would his love matter to her, as well?

He had to give it a try. He admired her independence, yet he still wanted to take care of her....

He had to focus, to get this right. He dropped to his knees on the concrete, smiling at the surprise on Sarah's face, then raised his hands and moved his fingers the way Adrianne had taught him and signed, "I love you, Sarah. I really love you. Will you marry me?"

Her eyes filled with tears. But wariness lingered as well.

He cupped her face in his hands and forced her to look at his mouth while he spoke. "This has nothing to do with pity or guilt or anything but the fact that the two of us belong together. I know you can take care of yourself, that you don't need me." Her eyes searched his face. "But *I* need you. And I want to take care of you because I love you." He placed her hands over his heart. "My heart can't go on without you, Sarah. Please marry me."

A slow smile lifted her lips. He was hoping, praying she would sign yes. Instead, she opened her mouth and said his name, "Adam." Then in the softest, sexiest, most sultry voice he could ever imagine, she whispered the word, "Yes."

Epilogue

Sarah smoothed down the satin edges of her wedding gown, then fastened her mother's locket around her neck, smiling as she thought of the photo she'd put inside. She'd added her father's picture beside her mother's. Now the locket signified her parents' love, and the love she would always share with her own husband.

Candlelight bathed the gazebo on the waterfront off the north end of Catcall Island, white lilies and lavender ribbons decorating the edges, creating a private canopy for the place they would say their vows. Ancient live oaks draped in Spanish moss filled the yard and the sunset colored the horizon, the beautiful oranges and reds a perfect backdrop for their ceremony today.

Adam stood inside the gazebo, his partner, Clay, beside him as his best man. Denise was her maid of honor, Adrianne another bridesmaid. Russell had agreed to give her away, bittersweet memories of Sol and her father surfacing as she took Russell's arm. But she wasn't going to let anything spoil her wedding day. And she had a surprise for Adam.

The guitarist began to play and Sarah tried to remember the way the chords had sounded when Adam strummed them.

She had Adam's voice imprinted there, too, the sound of his husky laughter, the memory of the erotic words he'd whispered in her ears, the sound of the waterfall in the background when they'd made love in that cave. And she would never forget it.

The next few minutes passed like a fairy tale. Finally, it was time to say their vows.

Adam clasped her hand in his and faced her, his dark eyes intense and soulful as his gaze met hers.

He kissed the palm of her hand, then laid it on his heart and released her. He signed and spoke at the same time. "Sarah, I once thought that love had no place in my life. But now I know that my life has no place without love in it. You taught me how to speak without words, how to listen with my heart and how to open myself up so I could have love. I love you today, I will love you tomorrow, I will love you always."

Sarah blinked back tears and took his hand in hers, then kissed his fingers in turn.

Finally, she cleared her throat and spoke slowly, watching the joy and surprise on his face as she pledged her own vows. "Adam, I lived in a world of silence most of my life, and was too afraid to speak out of fear of not being heard. But even without words, you heard my silent cries and understood. I will always treasure the memory of your voice, the sounds of the guitar as you played for me one night and the whisper of your breath when you call my name. I love you today, I will love you tomorrow and always."

They exchanged rings and Adam swept her into his arms for a soul-filled kiss.

Hours later, after they'd exhausted themselves with food and settled into one of the island cottages at the beach, Sarah lay naked in Adam's arms.

He cradled her face in his hands. "Hear me, Sarah, hear me whisper my love." As he rose above her and joined his body with hers, Sarah closed her eyes and heard the huskiness of his voice.

"I hear you, Adam." She threaded her fingers in his hair. "I thought you were going to finish that song when you said our vows."

He smiled and forced her to look into his eyes. "I haven't written the ending yet. I thought we'd write it together."

"I love you, Adam."

"I love you, too."

She kissed him thoroughly, then lowered her head to watch him move inside her. They had already begun to finish the song—they didn't need words to communicate at all.

Their love would bind them forever.

* * * * *

Look for Adam's partner Clay's story,
MEMORIES OF MEGAN,
coming soon only to Harlequin Intrigue.

TRUEBLOOD, TEXAS

Coming in May 2002...

RODEO DADDY

by

B.J. Daniels

Lost:

Her first and only love.
Chelsea Jensen discovers
ten years later that her father
had been to blame for
Jack Shane's disappearance
from her family's ranch.

Found:

A canceled check. Now Chelsea
knows why Jack left her. Had he ever loved her, or had she
been too young and too blind to see the truth?

Chelsea is determined to track Jack down and find out.
And what a surprise she gets when she finds him!

Finders Keepers: bringing families together

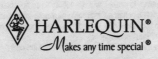

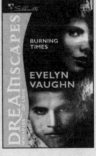
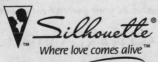

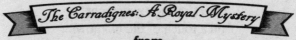
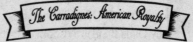